Books by Ellen Howard

Circle of Giving

When Daylight Comes

WHEN
DAYLIGHT
COMES

WHEN DAYLIGHT COMES

Ellen Howard

ATHENEUM   1985   NEW YORK

An immeasurable debt is owed to John L. Anderson and his
book, Night of the Silent Drums. The author thanks him
for his help and encouragement. Thanks also to Lito Valls,
U.S. National Park Service and to Stephen C. Edwards.

Library of Congress Cataloging in Publication Data

Howard, Ellen.   When daylight comes.

SUMMARY: After a slave uprising on an eighteenth
century settlement in the Virgin Islands, a white girl
held prisoner by the rebels follows a slow passage
to understanding of her captors.
1. Children's stories, American. [1. Slavery—Fiction.
2. Blacks—Fiction. 3. Revolutions—Fiction.
4. Virgin Islands of the United States—Fiction]
I. Title.
PZ7.H83274Wh 1985   [Fic]   85-7963
ISBN 0-689-31133-8

For Chuck, who found St. Jan for me.

"And not by eastern windows only,
  When daylight comes, comes in the light;
  In front, the sun comes slow, how slowly,
  But westward, look, the land is bright."

"Say Not the Struggle Naught Availeth"
ARTHUR HUGH CLOUGH

Contents

About This Story

In 1733, the tiny Caribbean island of St. Jan in the Virgin Islands (known now as St. John) was the scene of one of the most successful slave rebellions in the history of slavery in the Americas. It was led by three recently captive royal blacks: Bolombo, who had been a king of the Adampe tribe in Africa; Aquashi, who had been an Aquambo prince; and Kanta, a nobleman of the fierce Amina tribe. On the morning of November 23, 1733, their followers rose up against white masters all over the island. Many whites were killed; most of the rest fled from St. Jan.

The white masters were primarily Danish planters who, for about fifteen years, had been clearing the ancient lignum vitae forests of St. Jan to plant terraced fields of sugar cane and cotton. To do this, they had imported hundreds of slaves.

The first slaves on St. Jan were what was called

"accustomed" slaves, that is, people who had been born slaves of planters on other Caribbean islands. They knew no other way of life.

But in the late 1720s and early 1730s, the St. Jan planters bought many newly enslaved Africans, called "bussals," at the market at Tappus on the island of St. Thomas, the capital of the Danish West Indies. These slaves had been free black tribesmen before they were captured by African slave traders and sold to the European ships that landed on the Guinea coast. The bussals were crowded into the ships' holds and made to endure a many weeks voyage to the West Indies. Sometimes as many as half of them died of disease and suffocation and despair by the time they reached the slave markets.

The St. Jan planters took the bussals they purchased to their plantations, which they called "plantages," and set them to work. But the bussals were not the willing and docile workers the accustomed slaves had been. Some of them refused to work and were beaten or starved themselves to death. Many simply ran away and hid in those parts of the St. Jan forest not yet cleared for plantation.

The year 1733 was especially hard on St. Jan. A drought in the spring and summer damaged both the cotton and sugar cane crops, as well as the kitchen gardens. In July, a hurricane destroyed buildings and ruined more crops. Then, in the wake of the hurricane, grasshoppers descended on the last remaining fields and stripped them bare. Food was scarce. Slaves began to starve.

More and more of the slaves escaped into the forest to join the growing camps of runaways, called "marons." The drums of the marons began to beat every night, sending messages from camp to camp. Bolombo and Aquashi and Kanta began to plan how to save their people. The white planters grew afraid.

This is a story about the slaves' rebellion. All of the characters named in the story really lived, with three notable exceptions: Caroline, Lille, and "the little sore-eyed boy." But it is entirely possible that children like these were caught up in the terrible events of that time. The name "Lodama" was made up, because history does not record the African name of Bolombo's queen, but she was a real person, whose slave name was Judicia. The eleven-year-old daughter of St. Jan's magistrate was indeed named Helena. It is said she was killed on the first day of the rebellion.

But what if Helena had not been killed? What if she had been taken captive by the rebels? What if she had become their slave? This is a story that imagines the answers to those questions.

WHEN
DAYLIGHT
COMES

1

The Dreaming

Halfway between sleeping and waking, Helena began to feel something was wrong. Her nightgown was twisted hotly, damply around her legs. Her head was heavy and aching. The linen sheet was wet with her sweat.

She groped back down into comfortable sleep, searching among the events of the last few days for the something that was wrong. She dreamed . . . and she remembered. . . .

When the cannon had boomed from the fort last Saturday afternoon, Helena's grandfather jerked upright in his hammock so violently he was almost dumped out upon the gallery floor. He looked funny, clinging to the hammock's rocking sides with his pudgy hands and blinking, puffy-eyed, while he sputtered his alarm, and Helena began to laugh.

"It was the cannon only, Bedstefader," she said. "The cannon from the vaern."

But he did not hear her and sputtered more loudly.

Helena scrambled up from where she had been lying in the shade on the cool flagstones with a book and ran to look out over the railing. The gallery stretched the length of the upper story of the estate house, a long, shaded porch that afforded a view of the harbor and the little hill where the fort was built. The cannon boomed again. Its hollow sound hung in the hot, still air like the puff of smoke Helena saw rise lazily from Vaern Hill.

To the southeast, beyond Coral Bay, the tall masts and swelling sails of a large ship were clearing Bocken Island on the hazy, gray-blue sea. Helena squinted against the heat glare of water and sky to make her out. This was no ordinary inter-island barque or fishing boat. She was a koffardimand, a large well-armed merchantman. Heavy and proud, she rode the waves like a queen.

"Bedstefader, Bedstefader," Helena cried. "A big ship, a koffardimand comes!"

Bedstefader Gardelin was climbing out of his hammock, reaching precariously with his short legs for the gallery floor. His paisley banyan was wrinkled and soaked dark with sweat beneath the sleeves. His turban had been knocked askew so the tassel dangled between his eyes, and the grizzled stubble of his shaven head was plainly visible above one ear.

"A koffardimand? There is no merchant ship

expected. It cannot be a koffardimand, child!" he said, padding to the railing in his stockinged feet.

Helena's mother poked her head out of a window. She clutched her linen wrapping gown about her.

"What happens?" she cried, her face pinched and fearful. "Is it trouble with the slaves?"

"Nej, nej, Mama," Helena said. "The fort fires a salute to a ship passing by."

But her mother continued to peer wildly from her window.

The sound of bare feet slapping against stone floors could be heard inside the estate house as house slaves ran to look out of windows. Below, in the garden, a group of blacks huddled together, pointing toward the harbor and gabbling with excitement. Helena saw men run out of the Company warehouses on the waterfront to peer seaward, hands cupped over eyes. A bomba in the near field was shouting for the fieldhands to get back to work, but they ignored him until Helena heard the crack of his whip.

Bedstefader was shouting to Aero, his body slave, for a spyglass. Helena's mother was still crying and wringing her hands. Helena's baby brother, Thomas, was bellowing inside the house, and for once, no one paid him the slightest attention. All eyes were fixed on the sails, billowing white on the blurred blue horizon.

Helena climbed to the top of the low railing wall to see better over a clump of seagrape trees. She watched the ship, which seemed not to be sailing into the harbor, but past it, from the passage between St.

Jan and the Northman's island toward St. Thomas. How could there be enough wind to fill its sails, she wondered, when Helena felt no breath of moving air. Sweat trickled into Helena's eyes as she balanced on the railing. She thought how lovely it would be out there on the water with the wind blowing her hair from her perspiring neck and, perhaps, sea spray flung cool against her face. She could imagine standing by the ship's rail watching the sea slide by, and she thought what fun it would be to be sailing to someplace exciting, someplace with a town, perhaps, and a market and other girls her age.

Aero came running with Bedstefader's glass. Helena saw her grandfather snatch it from Aero's hand and raise it to his eye.

"It *is* a koffardimand!" he said, his shaggy eyebrows arching in surprise. "A big one."

"Ya," muttered Helena. "Ya, so I said."

But, once again, her grandfather seemed not to hear her. He squinted through the glass at the ship's flag.

"She's flying . . . she's flying Dannebrog!" he exclaimed. "She's a Danish merchantman, headed for St. Thomas."

Helena's mother had collapsed against the shutter, fanning her flushed and perspiring face with one plump hand and emitting shrill little cries of relief.

"A ship," her mother said. "A ship only, and those fools at the vaern firing to make a person think a catastrophe had befallen. They frightened me half out of my wits!"

"The vaern must salute the ship, Mama," said Helena.

She climbed from the gallery railing and plumped down on the top step, still gazing out to sea over the low balustrade. The ship was disappearing behind the point, the light of the low afternoon sun shining coral on its billowing sails.

Her grandfather was shouting to Aero to fetch his wig and his coat. A groom was sent scurrying to saddle a horse. Asari, the head house slave, could be heard relaying Bedstefader's orders to a runner to the fort. And all the while, Bedstefader paced the length of the gallery, alternately peering at the ship through his glass and yelling demands to hurry, hurry, hurry to the slaves.

"In Tappus I should be," he fumed. "The captain must be alerted I am not there, but visiting here. Why don't those idiots at the fort continue firing to get his attention?"

He clapped on his full-bottomed wig and wriggled impatiently into the stiff brocaded waistcoat and matching coat Aero held out for him, while at his feet another slave knelt to buckle his shoes.

Helena wondered at her grandfather's distress. He was the governor, after all, the most important man in the Danish islands, as her mother had told her many times. Surely the captain would wait for him if he was not at home in Tappus to greet the big ship when it anchored. Helena suspected Bedstefader was just anxious not to miss the excitement of the arrival of a ship from the homeland.

Bedstefader hurried past Helena, down the steps to the horse the groom was leading from the stables. Aero ran after him, almost tripping over Helena in his haste to help his master mount. In a moment, Helena was enveloped in a cloud of dust thrown up by the horse's hooves as Bedstefader kicked him into a gallop down the steep, curving drive that led to the road to the harbor. She lifted her linen petticoat away from her bare legs and flapped it to fan away the dust.

A koffardimand would bring supplies—salted meat and stockfish, butter and bread from Denmark, and countless other good things to eat. Helena hugged herself, thinking of what the ship might bring. A drought and a hurricane and a plague of insects had ruined the crops on St. Jan this year. There was little left to eat on the island. Helena had heard it said that, on some of the plantages, the slaves were starving. It was not so bad as that in Coral Bay, but Helena was tired of poorjack and watery gruel and an occasional stringy chicken made into soup.

Perhaps there would be cloth on the ship—chintz or dimity for a new frock or two. Helena was growing so fast her ankles showed beneath her petticoats despite the ruffles her mother had sewn around the hems.

Suddenly the vaern cannons began to speak again. *Boom. Boom. Boom.* The cannons were not firing an ordinary salute, but a steady round of shots, one after another, to catch the attention of the koffardimand. Helena saw the governor's flag—Bedstefader's flag, she thought with pride—go scampering up and down the fort flagpole. She peered at the place where the ship had disappeared and soon sighted the topsails coming into view again.

Helena jumped to her feet, a smile spreading on her face. Bedstefader would be so glad. The ship had seen his signal and had come about. She stood to, and Helena saw small white puffs of smoke spit over her port rail and heard the popping reports of her nine-gun salute to Governor Gardelin.

A lone mosquito shrilled past Helena's ear. Annoyed, she shook her head, but it circled closer, threatening to land and bite. She brushed the mosquito away with her hand. It hovered in the air above her head, whining, whining, *whining.* . . .

2

The Fever

*W*hining, *whining, a mosquito hummed mad-
deningly in Helena's ear. She tossed her head from
side to side on the pillow, fighting to stay asleep. In
that quiet hour just before dawn, when the tree frogs
and night insects had fallen silent and the birds had
not yet begun to sing, the whine of the mosquito was
the only sound in Helena's shuttered room. The silence
was part of the something that was wrong, but Helena
did not want to waken to find out what it was. She
wanted to dream about going with Bedstefader to St.
Thomas on the big ship. She was not ready to wake
from that dream. . . .*

"What about it, Reimo?" Bedstefader had asked
Helena's stepfather at supper last Saturday evening.

Helena watched Papa Sødtmann's face anxiously.
The light from the candles in their crystal chandelier
shone down on his high, domed forehead and

shadowed his jutting jaw and thoughtfully narrowed eyes. Helena saw a muscle jump near one corner of his mouth, and he let the silence stretch long, longer than Helena thought she could bear. He reached for the bowl of horseradish sauce and ladled a spoonful onto his plate. The candlelight glinted on the silver spoon and on his large gold signet ring. The ring was a symbol of Reimart Sødtmann's power as magistrate of St. Jan. With it, he sealed the fates of the people, both white and black, who came before his court.

Helena glanced at her mother and saw she had fixed her round blue eyes unblinkingly on her husband's face. She was twisting the ends of her neckerchief and biting her lips. Waiting for the verdict, Helena thought.

"A holiday would do Birgitta good, Reimo," Bedstefader said, and Helena's mother jumped nervously at the sound of his voice. "Tham and Willum would be delighted, I am sure, to have her and the children. Rebecca and her brood are visiting them even now. It could be a sort of reunion," Bedstefader said.

"It might be as well," Papa Sødtmann said. "I am sure there is no danger here, but even so . . . Would you like to visit your brothers, Birgitta?"

Helena's mother watched her husband's lips as intently as though she were reading them. "Oh, yes," she said, her voice small and breathless. "Oh, yes, if . . . if you wish it, my husband. I have been so frightened. That dreadful drumming every night . . . and the rumors. . . . They say the marons are gathering

arms . . . and the way the servants look at me . . ."
Her voice sank to a whisper, and her eyes flew to
Lorche, the kitchen maid, who stood in the corner,
head bowed and hands humbly folded.

"Nonsense," said Papa Sødtmann loudly.

At the sound of his voice, Mama seemed to shrink.

"I have said there is no danger. Those black
fools are children—running away from home out of
discontent. They haven't the brains to know it is
their masters who feed them, or the stomach to fight.
We are perfectly safe, so long as we take sensible
precautions. Nej, I was thinking of Thomas. The boy
grows old enough to benefit from the company of his
cousins. He is well over a year and begins to walk
and speak already. Rebecca's boys, the two younger,
would be good for him. He is too much with females
here."

Helena was trying to eat her soup as she listened
to Papa Sødtmann. Why could Mama not learn it was
important to behave as though the thing were *not*
wanted in order to get it from Papa Sødtmann? If he
thought they were anxious to go, he would be sure to
say they must stay. Helena lifted her spoon to her
mouth and drank off the soup as though the conversa-
tion were of no consequence to her, but her stomach
was roiling with anxiety, and the greasy smell of the
broth in her bowl made her sick.

"Quite so," said Bedstefader. "It would be well
to begin to visit other families with sons. A boy needs
male influences."

Inside herself, Helena smiled. Bedstefader was trying to help.

Mama was blinking hard, and Helena could see tears ready to spill over in her eyes. Don't cry, Mama, she willed silently. Please don't cry and spoil it.

"On the other hand," said Papa Sødtmann, "having Birgitta gone is most inconvenient to me." He spoke as though his wife were not sitting there. Helena's heart sank.

"Ya, ya," said Bedstefader. "Perhaps you are right. It is undoubtedly difficult to get along without a wife. I, myself, now that Birgitta's mother has passed on—"

"Very well," said Papa Sødtmann, suddenly interrupting him. "A short holiday can do no harm. Take Birgitta and the children with you tomorrow, Philip, as you please. A rest for me also it will be. A little peace and quiet for a change."

Mama's tears spilled over and ran down her plump, pink cheeks. Helena squeezed her eyes shut and took a deep, smiling, satisfied breath. Bedstefader was very clever, she thought, and Mama's tears could do no harm now. Papa Sødtmann has said they might go to visit Onkel Tham and Onkel Willum on St. Thomas Island. Against her closed eyelids, Helena envisioned the hustle-bustle marketplace of Tappus Town, the elegant estate house of her St. Thomas uncles, the short, thrilling voyage on the koffardimand. For that was perhaps the best part of all —they would sail tomorrow with Bedstefader on the koffardimand, which was waiting for him that moment in Coral Bay Harbor.

Helena opened her eyes and put down her spoon. She pushed her bowl of soup away, half-eaten. Her stomach heaved, and her face felt hot. It was the excitement that made her feel ill, she thought, the wonderful anticipation of tomorrow.

It was not the excitement.

By the next morning all of Helena's body ached with fever. When she tried to get up, her head swam so that she fell, and Caroline, her body slave, had to run to fetch Asari to lift her back onto the bed. Asari made Caroline stand at the head of the bed with a great palm-frond fan to stir the breeze. Lorche brought a basin of cool water to bathe Helena's forehead, while Asari went to tell Papa Sødtmann and Mama.

"I am going to St. Thomas today with my bedstefader," Helena told Caroline, the words stumbling thickly over her strangely clumsy tongue.

"Ya, ya, Missy," Caroline said, waving the fan back and forth, and her eyes were big and round and disbelieving.

Helena opened her mouth to protest she was indeed going to St. Thomas, but she saw Caroline's thin, black face receding from her, and the words would not come forth. "I am, I am going to St. Thomas today," Helena tried to cry just before she fell into darkness.

When she woke again, Helena's mother was hanging over her, wringing her hands. Papa Sødtmann was standing at the foot of the bed, his black brows drawn together. Bedstefader Gardelin stood near, his moon-shaped face distressed. Mester Bødker, the island's physician, was mixing a powder into a beaker of water on the brass and mahogany washstand. He turned toward the bed and held up the beaker to show them all.

"She must drink of this draught whenever she wakes," he was saying. "I will teach your servant to mix it, and I will come once a day to bleed and purge Helena. There is no cause for worry, Frue Sødtmann. These young people shake off fevers easily. She will be entirely recovered in a few days."

"A few days?" wailed Helena's mother.

"But to Tappus we must sail this very morning," said Bedstefader.

Helena tried to prop herself up on one elbow. She struggled against the linen sheet that had been pulled up under her chin. It seemed as heavy as a mattress piled on top of her, and as hot. The room tipped from side to side. For a single dizzy moment, she wondered if she was already on the koffardimand, sailing to St. Thomas.

"I am going . . . I am going to St. . . . . Thomas," Helena said, and she felt Mester Bødker's big hand pushing her firmly back onto her pillow.

"Drink this," he said, and held the beaker to her lips and tipped the bitter liquid into her mouth, which was open to protest. Helena choked on the nasty potion running down her throat.

"You will have to go without her," Mester Bødker said to Bedstefader. "Helena will not be able to travel for at least a week."

"A week!" cried Helena's mother, casting her eyes frantically from the doctor to her husband to Bedstefader as though in search of another opinion.

Bedstefader shook his head. "I must go this morning," he said. "The ship waits for me."

"I cannot leave her?" said Helena's mother, and even Helena heard the question in her voice.

A lump came into Helena's throat as she understood what was going to happen. Mama wanted to go so badly, Helena knew. The drums and rumors frightened her. It was not that she wanted to leave Helena behind. Helena knew that. It was just she was so fearful. Sometimes Helena thought Mama acted as young as Thomas, who knew only to cry for what he wanted.

"Lorche can take care of her," said Papa Sødtmann. "When she is well, I will send her over on the first barque to Tappus."

"But will she be all right?" said Mama. She was patting Helena's arm. Letting me know she loves me, Helena thought.

"The fever is not serious," said Mester Bødker.

"I have told you, there is absolutely no danger from the marons," said Papa Sødtmann. "Would I be staying if there were?"

Helena could feel tears rolling down her cheeks, hotter even than her burning skin.

"You will be all right, kjaereste, dearest one?" Helena's mother said, looking into her eyes. She took a lace-edged handkerchief from her pocket and patted away Helena's tears. "Kjaereste?" she said.

Helena nodded wearily and turned away her face, wishing suddenly they would all go away and leave her alone.

"Ya," she said. "Ya, Mama. I will be all right."

It was Caroline's task to fan Helena. Sometimes she stood at the head of the bed. Sometimes, when no one else was about, Helena would wake to find her sitting on the pillow beside her. Caroline switched the fan from hand to hand and often, in the heat of the afternoon or deep in the night, she fell asleep and dropped the fan. But much of the time, in the days of illness that followed the departure of Bedstefader and Mama and Thomas, Helena could feel the pleasant stirring of the air in the wake of Caroline's fan. It cooled her a little and eased the aching of her feverish skin. She liked the feeling of the soft air moving over her face and body as the fan waved to and fro, *to and fro. . . .*

3

The Nightmare

To and fro, Caroline's fan would stir the air over Helena as she slept, cooling her and keeping the mosquitoes away.

That was what was wrong, Helena realized even before she opened her eyes. There was no gentle breeze of air moving across her sweaty body. That lazy girl must have fallen asleep again! Helena's eyes opened and she started to call Caroline's name. But even as she opened her mouth, she realized she was alone in her gauze-draped bed, alone in the dark and the unnatural quiet.

For some reason, Helena felt unwilling to move. Her arms and legs were tense and heavy. She found she was holding her breath, listening, listening . . . and searching the darkness with her eyes. Had she had a bad dream? Sometimes, waking from a nightmare, she felt this fear. It held her motionless, as though to move might bring disaster.

Nothing broke the stillness—no sound of animals or insects, of servants or Papa Sødtmann, no sound of dawn-singing birds. Helena willed herself to breathe and gradually felt her pounding heart quiet. Cautiously, she stretched her legs and turned toward the window.

Around the wooden shutters, bands of faintest gray broke the blackness. It must be near dawn, Helena thought. She sat up in bed. Her skin felt sweaty and cooled by the sweat, not dry and feverish as it had been for so many days. Mester Bødker had been right last evening when he said she was almost recovered.

Helena cocked her head to listen. In a moment, a bird would trill, or the bantam cock would crow. In a moment, the conch-shell tutu would sound, calling the slaves to wake and begin another day. She listened and heard none of these things.

It was a muttering she heard, so faint at first she wondered if she only imagined it.

The muttering grew louder. Was it voices? Voices held low? And feet shuffling along the passage floor? Helena heard pounding at a wooden door near hers. The muttering ceased. There was a voice, Papa Sødtmann's voice, thick with sleep, and then Helena heard Asari speak. She leaned back against the pillow, relaxing with relief. It was only Asari, come to waken Papa Sødtmann for some reason.

Helena liked Asari. Often, he smiled at her and spoke to her gently in his excellent Danish. He was tall and handsome, a "Malagasy," Papa said, with long, straight black hair and a slender, straight-held back that made Helena think him strong and digni-fied. Papa Sødtmann had made him chief of their house slaves because he was so quick and clever and because his education made him, as Papa said, "almost civilized." It was Asari who had seen that Helena was bathed every day to cool her fever, that she was given the freshest bread, the hottest soup, the best of things to eat while she was ill. It was Asari who learned how to mix her healing draught, and who, with gentle hands, had lifted her up to drink it and given her lumps of sugar afterwards to hold on her tongue until the nasty taste was gone.

Helena decided to get up and ask Asari where Caroline was. Heedless girl, Caroline had orders to stay by Helena's side and see to her comfort! Asari would set her right with a cuff of his big brown hand.

Helena put her feet over the edge of the high mahogany bed, parting the gauze mosquito bar with one hand, and slid to the floor. She could hear Papa Sødtmann's door being unbolted. Papa Sødtmann was saying something. Helena heard his voice, heard the anger in it. She was reaching for her wrapper when she heard the scream.

It rent the dawn-lit air, harsh and throbbing like the squeal of a butchered pig, and ended suddenly in a strangling sound. Helena dived back onto the bed, tangling herself in the gauze, and clutched the bedpost fast as though to keep from falling. The passage was filled with noise now—voices and running footsteps and the clank and crash of metal, shouts and cries and, above them, the babble of the voice that had screamed.

"Nej, nej," the voice cried. "I have been a good master. You have no right."

Helena's heart seemed to stop. The voice was Papa Sødtmann's.

Helena had crawled to the farthest edge of the bed. Her head was buried beneath the pillow. She had pulled the sheets up and curled as small as she could make herself. She could not think. The terrible sounds went on and on. Twice the cannons boomed from the fort. She could not make out their meaning. Three shots was the signal for the planters to arm against trouble. Two shots meant nothing—not a salute or a signal or even enough firing to indicate defense of the fort. Helena stopped her ears. She wanted only to go back to sleep and wake again when the tutu sounded and the cock began to crow, wake again to the smell of food cooking and to Lorche bringing her breakfast on a tray and to the breeze of Caroline's fan.

And then her door burst open, and there was the sound of feet pounding across her floor, and her sheets were ripped away, and she lay exposed to the hands that seized her and lifted her from her bed.

He was hurting her! How dare he hurt her! Lay his dirty hands upon her? How dare he? Helena began to scream and beat upon his back with her fists as he flung her over his shoulder. His back was black and gleaming with sweat and his smell was strong and acrid in her nose. His arms held her legs across his chest in a pitiless grip, and he laughed at the blows she dealt him and hit her hard across the buttocks and laughed again.

Helena struggled and tried to kick her legs. The slave was carrying her from her room and down the passage. She twisted her body to see where she was being carried and saw the brightness of flambée-stoks casting weird black shadows ahead of them against the passage walls. She did not know the slave who was carrying her. He was not one of theirs. What was he doing in her house? He had no right to be there. Between dusk and dawn slaves were forbidden to leave their own plantages.

"You will be punished!" she gasped. "Put me down immediately or I will have you punished!"

The slave only laughed again, a deep, ugly laugh that frightened Helena more. Where was Papa Sødtmann? The memory of the awful, babbling voice came to her mind, and she put it away from her. That could not have been Papa Sødtmann, she thought. *He* was strong and fierce.

The slave swung her off his shoulder and set her on her feet. If he had not been holding her tightly, one hand gripping her shoulder with biting fingers, the other twisted cruelly in her hair, she might have fallen, the room spun so crazily. Everywhere, in the

dimness, Helena saw black faces alight with something terrifying in their eyes. Black bodies shoved their
ways through the door from the gallery and crowded
close behind Helena and her captor. Their smell was
hot and heavy in the room, and Helena wanted to
retch. Frantically, she searched the faces for help.

There was Papa's bomba, Juni, his high-cheeked
face twisted in a grimace, his mouth open to shout
something Helena could not hear over the din. In the
hand he brandished overhead was a cane knife that
caught the light of flambée-stoks held high in other
hands.

The Company's Philip—Helena recognized him
as a runner who sometimes brought messages to Papa
—had jumped upon a table in the middle of the room
and was hacking again and again with an ax at something lying there.

They were in the dining room, Helena realized.
The crystal chandelier that was Mama's pride swung
on its chain, unlit, above the table until Philip, annoyed by its swinging near his head, reached up and
wrenched it from the ceiling and smashed it on the
floor. Slave women fell upon the brilliant prisms of
shattered glass, gathering them up with delighted
cries, unmindful of the cuts the glass made in their
hands. Other women were tearing down the velvet
draperies at the windows and wrapping the cloth
around their bodies, laughing and, Helena saw, some
of them were crying, tears running down their shining
cheeks as they stroked the rich, soft cloth. Whatever

will Mama say, Helena thought, when she comes back, to see her lovely things ruined?

Helena felt her captor's grasp relax and twisted frantically to escape him. He hit her so hard on the side of the head her ear buzzed, and dazed, she put her hand to it and felt the wetness of her own blood. Her legs gave out beneath her, and the excruciating pain in her head told her she hung by her hair from his hand.

And then she saw Asari. He was just in front of them. She scrambled to get her feet beneath her once again and cried as loudly as she could, "Asari! Asari, make them stop. Papa Sødtmann will be so angry! He will put them on the rack if they do not stop at once!"

Asari's face loomed before her. Hopefully, she reached out to him, and then her arms fell to her sides. She had never seen him like this before. The gentleness was gone from his eyes. His hand gripped a knife, smeared red and wet, and the redness was splashed on his green livery coat and even on his chin. He glared at her as though he had never seen her before. He snatched her from her captor and hurled her at the table.

"Master shall never put a black man on the rack again," he cried, and jerking her head up by her hair, he shoved her face toward the thing on the table. "Never again," he said. "Never again."

Helena heard ugly laughter behind her. Philip stopped hacking at the thing on the table. He crouched back, grinning, and displayed it to Helena. The wet redness was everywhere. Helena saw a hand in the heap on the table. Its skin was white and smeared with red, and on one hairy finger was a ring. Helena's eyes widened and her mouth opened and she heard someone scream as she recognized it. It was Papa Sødtmann's signet ring. The screaming went on and on until it carried her into darkness.

4

The Awakening

This time Helena was truly awake. There was no pretending it was a dream. The pain that smashed through her side was real, and the pandemonium that surrounded her was real, and Asari, most of all Asari, was real, standing above her, his eyes fierce, kicking her awake.

"You, Missy," he said, and his voice did not sound like Asari's voice at all, "you go with them." He pulled her to her feet and pushed her toward a group of women slaves. "We go to meet King Bolombo," he ordered. "If Missy does not keep up, you will know what to do." He thrust his knife into the hand of a woman wearing Mama's old straw hat set backwards on her head and strode away into the throng of men shoving their ways out onto the gallery.

The woman gazed down at the knife in her hand, and then she wiped the blade carefully on her apron and tested it for sharpness against her thumb. She was grinning when she looked up at Helena, a wide, gap-toothed grin, and Helena realized the face beneath Mama's hat was Lorche's.

"You shall come, Missy," Lorche said, moving the knife menacingly toward Helena. The other women laughed. Helena grabbed the table edge to keep from falling, and her fingers slipped on its wetness. She tried to catch her breath against the pain that burned in her side where Asari had kicked her and nodded, gasping, too hurt and surprised to cry. Lorche jerked her away from the table, and Helena was careful not to look back at it. She pushed out of her mind the vision of what lay on top of it and concentrated on drawing one hurting breath after another as she was shoved and jostled through the muttering crowd by the women.

Out on the gallery, Helena saw that the sun had risen over Buscagie Hill. Its golden glow touched the faces of the slaves and took away their wild and frantic looks. Now they seemed like the faces of people hurrying to a party, except that here and there Helena saw gory smears on their cheeks or chins and browning stains on their rags. Helena recognized her family's clothes on some of them. A crippled laundry slave wore one of Thomas's little petticoats about her shoulders like a cape. Helena saw Caroline in her own pink lawn frock. And, of course, Mama's flat straw hat, tied with blue ribbons, dipped and swayed atop Lorche's woolly head.

At the top of the stairs, Helena craned her head

around an old woman who clutched at her arm, pulling her along, and tried to see down to the road and harbor below. Surely the soldiers would come soon from the fort to stop this! She caught her breath hopefully at the sight of figures streaming from Vaern Hill and squinted her eyes to see them better. But their skins shone black and naked in the morning sun, and she heard a gombee drum pulsing on the breeze. Her knees gave way, and she almost fell.

The old woman and Lorche held Helena up and forced her down the stairs. The column of people poured out of the house and carried her along. Once, she looked ahead and saw they were led by Juni, who danced back and forth across the road, flourishing a pole over his head. Before Helena let herself realize what was impaled upon the pole, she dropped her gaze to the ground at her feet.

Dimly, Helena was aware that the two groups of slaves met upon the road near the beach. Helena's group greeted the slaves from the fort with songs and cries. Some of the women wept and repeated over and over again the name Asari had said.

"Bolombo! Bolombo! Bolombo!" they cried. They danced and chanted and, merging, the two groups headed into the sun along the road toward Mester Bødker's house. Up ahead, the men marched, and the sunlight reflected cruelly off their weapons into Helena's eyes. Behind them came the women, laughing, singing, and shouting jests at one another, and with them, the children. Babies were slung on mothers' backs, and Helena saw skinny boys and girls in ragged shirts dart through the line of people, throwing rocks and shouting. In the midst of the women, Helena staggered in her white nightgown.

Her heart lifted hopefully when they reached Mester Bødker's house. She waited to hear his voice firmly order the slaves to disperse. But Mester Bødker did not appear. There seemed to be no white people in the house, but only another small group of marauding slaves, who welcomed the newcomers' aid in flinging chairs and tables through the windows and smashing crockery on the ground. Lorche left Helena in the old woman's charge in the shade of a mampoo tree to join the looters in the house.

It was cool beneath the tree. Helena sat, her head drooping on her arms, and tried to shut out the noises in her head. Where was everybody? Where could everyone be? And when an answering vision came to her, of the bloody thing on the table at home, she refused to look at it and made her mind empty and numb. She closed her eyes, and the noises from Mester Bødker's house seemed faint and far away, and even the pain in her side and ache in her head were vague and meaningless.

Lorche returned and prodded Helena to her feet, and the march began again.

At the grigri tree near Suhm's, the rebels paused. A tall man, his shining skin tatooed from face to feet— like black brocaded satin, Helena thought—strode back through the crowd of men, who made way for him respectfully. He stood before the women and spoke to them in a language Helena did not understand. His voice was deep and commanding, and the women were silent, listening to him. When he had finished speaking, he disappeared again into the men, dividing them with waves of his hand into two groups. One went back toward the fort. The other group he led himself away from the women, who squatted obediently under the grigri tree and seemed to be waiting. Helena realized some of the women had not understood the words of the tatooed man, for others were explaining to them in the Dutch Creole tongue most of the slaves spoke.

"Bolombo say womans them wait here," Lorche told the old woman.

"Bolombo takes loot for mans," the old woman grumbled, but she squatted beneath the grigri tree and undid the bundle she had been carrying on her back.

Helena had fallen where they stopped. She slumped there, staring dully as the women settled themselves to wait. Some had brought food, which was shared out among the rest, and they chatted and laughed as though on a picnic. No one offered Helena anything to eat, but she did not care. She lay down, her cheek against the ground. The gnats swarmed about her face, and she was too tired to brush them away.

A small brown lizard advanced cautiously to within a few inches of her face and fixed its jewel-bright eyes upon her and flared its ruddy throat in challenge. When she did not move, it set about capturing the gnats with its flashing tongue.

With unfocused eyes, Helena comprehended its presence. She did not care. She did not think.

She did not know how long a time had passed before Lorche pulled her to her feet again, but this time, when they set out, there were only four of them. Lorche and the old woman took turns prodding her along. Caroline followed behind.

At first, the flat cobblestones of the wide Konge Vej, the King's Highway, passed beneath Helena's stumbling feet. But at Suhm's, the well-paved road turned into a rutted wagon trail as the women turned inland and began to climb steeply over the ridge toward the north shore.

The pain in Helena's bare feet was beginning to supplant the ache of her side and head. She was not used to walking barefooted, and the trail was rough with rocks that bruised her tender heels and cut into her feet with their jagged edges. The ground was growing hot as the sun rose in the sky. Helena raised one foot after the other and set it down, bracing each time for the agony that shot up her leg from the foot on the ground. She began to stagger drunkenly. Her legs got twisted in her long nightgown, and thorny fingers of catch-and-keep growing at trail's edge reached out to clutch and hold her.

Finally, Lorche jerked her roughly to a halt. She grabbed the hem of Helena's gown and ripped it up the seam and tied the two ends around Helena's waist. It was easier to walk after that, the gown covering her only to mid-thigh, but now the catch-and-keep tore at her bare legs. Helena's blood mixed with her sweat. She was bathed in moisture, and her hair was wet on the back of her neck, and stinging rivulets ran into her eyes. Her head pounded in cadence to the leaping torment of her feet.

At each plantage they passed, the women paused to search for loot, and they grumbled at the little left by Bolombo's men; but they gathered up whatever food they could find and filled goatskins and calabashes with water from cisterns and rain barrels. Helena saw no white man or woman on the way, not at Suhm's or Hendrichsen's or Castan's. At the estate house of her Onkel Peder Krøyer, there was another blood-soaked heap of rags at the foot of the stairs to the house, from which Helena averted her eyes.

When the women would let her rest, she fell to the ground and lay there motionless until they heaved her up again. Her throat became clogged with dust, and her lips swelled and split. When she begged for water, the old woman poured a gourd of water over her face, and she gulped and choked on what she could catch in her mouth and licked the water from her lips while the old woman screeched her high-pitched laugh.

Near Stallart's plantage, they met a group of bearers coming back along the trail.

"King Bolombo headquarters at Waterlemon

Bay," their leader said. "We moving his camp from van Stell's Point."

"Where's Bolombo's womans?" Lorche asked.

"The queen waits at Waterlemon Bay," said the leader.

"Good," said Lorche, pushing Helena forward. "We bring the queen a slave."

5

The Queen

By the time the women straggled down the trail and into the encampment at the Waterlemon Bay plantage, Helena was barely conscious. Lorche and the old woman dragged her between them. She no longer tried to lift her feet, but let them trail along the uneven ground. Her chin bumped against her chest, and her hair had fallen over her face in pale, wet strands. Her eyes were closed.

The first thing she knew was the release of the grip that pained her shoulders, and the welcome fall to the ground. There was stone beneath her face, and it felt cool to her cheek. She sought unconsciousness and release from pain and felt angry when a hand grasped her chin and waked her, turning her face to one side and brushing the hair from her eyes.

"A slave too weak to stand no good," a voice above her said in the Creole slave tongue. The words were angry, but the voice was soft and rich, and a little sad. "You shall carry her to the others," the voice said. "See they get water and what food we can spare. I decide by and by about them."

The hand rested a moment longer on Helena's head, gentle and comforting. Helena heard the words, "the others," and her heart leaped with hope. Others must have been brought to this place. She tried to rise as the rough, hurting hands pulled at her again. She tried to walk, to stumble between them as they led her away. But now she could not keep the blackness from overwhelming her. She had prayed for it, and now, too late, it came. She slumped unconscious between the women who carried her.

"I think she be waking," said a voice.

" 'Lena, be you waking up?"

Painfully, Helena stirred her arms and legs. She groaned. The slightest movement sent pain racing through her body and pounding behind her eyes.

" 'Lena? 'Lena? Be you waking up?"

Helena opened her eyes, and in the dim light from a low doorway, she saw Peter Minnebeck's face close to hers.

She moved her lips, trying to speak, and heard a strange kind of croaking come from her mouth.

"Peter?" She tried again. "Peter Minnebeck, is it truly you?"

His face split in a wide grin. "Ya, ya, 'tis me. Me 'n Hans. We thought you were dead."

Hans's face appeared beside Peter's, almost

identical, with a fringe of flaxen hair and pale blue eyes. Hans was grinning too.

Hans and Peter Minnebeck were Mester Bødker's stepsons. Peter was a little older than Helena, Hans almost two years younger. They were the nearest neighbor children, and Helena had always envied them, for they were allowed to do all the things Papa Sødtmann and Mama said a young lady ought not to do. They swam and rowed their little boat in the bay whenever they pleased and roamed at will through the bush or on the beach. They hung around the warehouses and the fields and the sugar boiling sheds. Peter had a gun he didn't like to use, but Hans used it often, bringing down doves and parakeets for practice. And no one reprimanded them when *they* were noisy or rambunctious.

"Told you she wasn't dead," said Hans.

Painfully, Helena sat up and looked around her. Peter held out a wooden trencher of water, and she took it from him and drank. The water stung her lips, but was wet on her parched tongue, and she found herself gulping it. It ran out the sides of her mouth, and Peter put out a gentle hand to restrain her.

"Slowly now," he said. "It be all we have."

Helena took another gulp and held the water in her mouth, savoring it and letting it seep slowly down her throat. She handed the trencher back.

"We have some bread," said Hans, and held out a coarse gray lump to her.

She shook her head. The water was roiling uncomfortably in her stomach. She turned her head and gazed about.

They were in a small hut, so low they could not stand upright, so narrow that, lying down stretched out, she could reach from wall to wall with her hands and feet. The strong odor Helena associated with field slaves permeated the hot, rancid air of the hut, mixed with the rotting, dusty smell of the palm-thatched roof. Through holes in the thatch, she could see the sky. It was the deep, bright blue of afternoon.

Helena looked at Hans and Peter. Apparently, they had been allowed to dress, for they wore shirts and breeches and shoes. Their clothes were not so ripped and dirty as her gown, nor did they appear to be hurt.

"I was at your house," said Helena. "They took me to your house, but I did not see you or your father. Where were you?"

"Moth's Aero and Schønnemann's Christian and some others took us from our beds before light and brought us here," Hans said.

"You did not see our Papa Bødker?" Peter said.

Helena shook her head.

"They would not kill him," said Hans, almost fiercely. "You be wrong, Peter. They need him to heal their wounded."

Peter shook his head slowly. "I have seen no wounded," he said, his voice so low Helena could barely hear him.

"There will be wounded," said Hans. "We were

taken by surprise, but soon our people will fight back, and then there *will* be wounded. It will all be over by tomorrow. But, in the meanwhile, they have spared Papa Bødker. He has always doctored them. They know his value to them."

Peter was still shaking his head, but he leaned forward and put his hand on Helena's. "What of your people, 'Lena?" he said.

"Mama and Thomas went to Tappus with my bedstefader last week. Papa Sødtmann . . . Papa Sødtmann . . ." The vision of the table rose before her eyes; she pushed it away and clamped her mouth shut. She could not say it. But she did not need to.

Peter said, "Never mind, 'Lena," in a gentle voice, and Hans said, "Dead."

Outside the hut, there were voices, and then the doorway was darkened as a head and shoulders thrust their way in.

"You shall come," said the man, and he backed out again.

Helena and Peter and Hans looked at one another. Then, without saying anything, Hans crawled to the doorway. Stiffly, Helena followed him, with Peter helping her.

"Bow down to the queen," the man said, shoving them roughly to their knees on the walkway in front of the Waterlemon Bay overseer's house.

Helena peeked up through her hair at the woman sitting cross-legged above them on the gallery. She was a big brown woman, naked except for a scarlet cloth knotted about her hips and a lady's bodice of yellow silk, much too small, worn like a vest. She held her head proudly and high. Her arms and legs were liberally tatooed, and the tatoos coiled in intricate, raised designs across her broad cheeks. Above the tatooed cheeks, two large brown eyes appraised Helena and the boys.

"I Lodama," she said, and Helena recognized her voice as the one belonging to the gentle hand of a while ago. "I the wife of Bolombo," the woman said.

"I know you," said Hans. "You be Castan's Judicia. You used to belong to Herre Krøyer."

Helena looked up at the woman again, sharply. Hans was right. Helena knew the woman too, for Peder Krøyer was Helena's uncle.

"I Lodama," the woman repeated firmly, "wife of Bolombo, the king."

"King of what?" said Hans, though Peter was jabbing him in the side with an elbow, trying to keep him quiet.

Another woman stepped forward, out of the deep shade of a doorway. She was as richly black as Judicia was brown, and she held a cane knife, which she slashed through the air above the children's heads.

Helena covered her head with her arms and cowered before the fierce glint of her black eyes. The boys cringed. The woman glared and stepped back.

A little smile played about Judicia's lips.

"Please, Judi . . . Please, Lodama . . . *Queen* Lodama," Peter said, his voice shaking, "what has happened to our stepfather?"

"The king . . . the *king of this island* say Mester Bødker shall be spared. All other masters die."

"And . . . and us? What about us?"

"You servants of the king and queen. You well treated."

"You haven't treated Helena very well," said Hans, his voice rising hotly. "Just look at her."

Judicia's eyes moved to Helena. "Little missy alive," she said.

"Half alive," muttered Hans, and Peter jabbed him in the ribs again.

Judicia's voice rose commandingly, and the fierce black woman leaned forward again, punctuating the pronouncement with thrusts of her heavy cane knife.

"Hear Lodama, little Masters, little Missy," Judicia said. "King Bolombo spares you. King Bolombo *owns* you, and you live because he not kill you. No more little masters. No more little missy. Slaves. You slaves now. You shall think on it."

She nodded her head to the man who had brought them out to her, and he stepped forward and motioned for them to rise. As she turned, Helena saw that Judicia had closed her eyes and leaned her head back against the gallery wall. The fierce black woman had stepped back into the shadows. On either side of the queen knelt a slim brown girl, gently waving a palm-frond fan.

6

Asari

Just after dawn of the second day, they took Hans and Peter away. When Helena tried to follow them out of the hut, she was shoved roughly back. She did not see them again.

She cried, feeling sick and desolate, and after a while she slept again. From time to time, she roused. Once there was an uproar outside. People ran back and forth, shouting, and she heard the wailing of women, and the gombee drums began to beat. When quiet came again, it was quieter than before. She did not hear the laughter and talk of the women, and the children did not run about playing. Once in a while through the haze of pain that fogged her mind, she heard a baby cry.

She had finished the water in the wooden trencher. They did not bring her food.

The sun was high overhead, making the little hut

an airless oven, when the drums began again. At first, Helena heard them faintly in the distance, and then they answered from within the camp. She heard men's voices, speaking in the slave language, and the sound of running feet. And then she heard Asari's voice, giving orders in the same peremptory tone he used when he commanded house slaves.

Helena crawled to the doorway of the hut and looked out. She could see a scattering of other slave huts, most larger and in better repair than hers. Women, or sometimes old men, squatted in the doorways of the huts. Their faces were grim and fearful. When a baby, crawling in the dust of a dooryard, began to cry, his mother reached out a pale-palmed hand and clamped it across his mouth.

An old man leaned against the wall of Helena's hut, his eyes half closed. With a grass whisk, he waved away the little stinging flies.

Helena heard Asari's voice grow nearer. In a moment, he came in sight around the bend in the path. A group of men followed close behind.

Asari no longer wore his green livery coat, of which Helena had thought him so proud. He wore only a loincloth, torn, Helena could see, from a woman's petticoat, for there were remnants of lace about its edge, a delicate white tracery against the deep mahogany of Asari's skin. He stopped before her hut, and Helena drew back into the shadows.

"Come with me," said Asari in his commanding tone. He was speaking in Danish.

Helena's heart began to thump.

"Come with me, I say," he said, and bent and reached out his arm for her and dragged her from the hut. He looked at her, and Helena wanted to beg him to help her but knew, with an angry sense of betrayal, that there was no help from him.

She struggled to stand up.

He turned abruptly and strode up the path again without glancing back at her.

Helena hobbled after him as fast as the pain in her feet would allow.

Asari said something over his shoulder to the group of men. One of them stepped forward and hoisted Helena over his shoulder. The other men melted away in several directions. Trotting, Helena's bearer followed Asari back toward the main buildings.

Helena did not protest being carried. However humiliating it was to be flung like a sack over the shoulder of a black slave, it was better than walking on her lacerated feet.

At the overseer's house, Helena was carried into a storage room on the lower level and dumped in a heap on the floor. Again Asari spoke to the bearer, and the man retreated through the door. Helena and Asari were alone in a small, cool room with a stone floor and thick whitewashed walls and a single high, barred window.

Helena sat up, rubbing an elbow that had been bumped when she was dropped on the floor. After the glare of outdoors, the room was so dim she could see only a shadow where Asari stood near the doorway, watching after the bearer. She heard, more than saw, him turn swiftly toward her and felt him kneel at her side. His strong hands ran gently over her body, and she winced when he touched her aching side.

Asari sighed and squatted back on his heels.

"Good," he said in Danish. "Missy is not badly hurt."

"You kicked me," said Helena. "It's you who hurt me."

Asari's voice was very quiet. "Missy lives," he said. "It was necessary to hurt you so you might live."

Helena blinked, trying to understand what he was saying. His voice was the voice she remembered, gentle and kind.

"Listen well to me, Missy," Asari said, and Helena thought it sounded like a plea, rather than a command. "You must do as I say. The bussals want to kill all the white people. Men, women, even children. The bussals say white children grow into white masters. I told them a white child can be a slave of black people. A white child can work for black masters as black children have worked for white masters. I made the bussals think this is a good revenge."

"But why did you hurt me?" Helena said. "You didn't have to hurt me." Her head was spinning. Was Asari, after all, the friend she had thought him to be?

"The bussals must think Asari hates Missy," he said.

"But . . . but Papa Sødtmann. You let them k . . . k . . . kill Papa Sødtmann."

Helena's eyes had adjusted to the dimness of the room. She could see Asari's face harden.

"Master was a bad man," he said shortly, rising. "You never mind about Master. You listen to Asari now."

Helena gulped back her tears and nodded her head, subdued by his voice.

Asari towered over her, tall and powerful and commanding. "King Bolombo lies wounded," Asari said. "Badly wounded." He jerked his head toward the ceiling and Helena realized he meant the bussal king lay upstairs, in the overseer's house. "The drums say Mester Bødker is coming. He will be here soon."

Helena caught her breath in sharply. "Is he coming to get us?" she said. "Is he coming to get Hans and Peter and me?"

Asari shook his head. "The Minnebeck boys are gone. The queen set them free. She said these are sons of a good man. She said Mester Bødker shall heal Bolombo. So she set his sons free."

"But what about me?" said Helena. "Why didn't she set me free?"

"Missy is the daughter of a bad man, the queen says. Missy shall be a slave, or Missy shall die."

Helena swallowed hard. She remembered the firm voice of Judicia. "You slaves now," Judicia had said. "You shall think on it."

Asari leaned forward, and his voice was urgent. "You must stay here. You must make no sound. *No sound.* If Mester Bødker knows you are here, they will surely kill you—and him as well. Do you understand? The bussals will surely kill you both, and I will be powerless to save you."

Helena nodded.

Asari put his hand gently on her arm. "No sound," he said.

And then, swiftly, he rose and was gone, the heavy door banging shut behind him. Helena heard the sound of the bolt being shot. She was alone again, and this time she was locked in.

Helena strained her ears for sounds to tell her what was happening. The band of light from the high window moved across the floor and widened to a square as the sun traveled past midday. In the coolness of the storeroom, her head cleared. She could gather together her thoughts. Little by little, she comprehended all that had happened to her since she had awakened the day before in her own bed.

She crawled to the square of light from the window and examined her arms and legs. Asari was right. Although she was badly bruised, nothing was broken. She ran her fingers through her tangled hair, trying to smooth it a bit, and pushed it behind her ears. She rubbed away the crusted blood in her ear and on her neck. The ear ached, but it was not bleeding now. Where Asari had kicked her in the side, her ribs were tender, but the stabbing pain when she breathed had dulled to a throb. Her feet were the worst. They were swollen, crusted with blood, and bruised black on the soles. They had never been so filthy.

She made a face to think what Mama would say if she could see those feet, and at the thought of Mama,

a lump rose in her throat. She fought back tears.
Mama could not help me, even if she were here. I
must help myself, thought Helena. She looked down
at her gown, torn and filthy, stiff with blood and dirt
and sweat. She set about pulling its drawstrings
tighter around her throat and retying them, and she
untied the torn tails of the gown Lorche had fastened
around her waist. The gown was ripped almost to her
armpit on one side, but she tied together some of the
threads dangling from the torn edge to hold it loosely
closed. It was the best she could do until she could find
a clean frock. And some water, Helena thought. What
I truly need is water—water for washing and water to
drink. And food. It was the first time she had thought
of food, and suddenly she was ravenous. No wonder I
feel so weak, she thought. I have not eaten for almost
two days.

There were some wooden crates stacked in one
corner of the storeroom. Beside them stood a wooden
keg. Helena pulled herself up, holding to the wall,
and limped toward the corner, hoping there might be
food. At the same time, she heard the *clop-clop* of
horse's hooves on the hard-packed dirt of the estate
roadway.

The window was too high. Even standing on tip-
toe, the top of her head would not reach the sill. She
looked for a chair or table to stand upon. Nothing. She
looked at the crates, but they were a long way from
the window, and when she tugged at one, she realized
they were too heavy to move.

The hoofbeats were growing closer, and she could

hear Asari's voice, and then Mester Bødker answered.
Without conscious thought, she tipped over the heavy
keg and rolled it beneath the window. Then, after
tipping it upright again, she climbed upon it. Standing on the keg, she could just reach the bars of the
window with her hands. She grasped them and pulled
herself up, panting, until her eyes came above the
windowsill. She could see nothing but a tall clump of
grass growing near the foot of the stairs leading to a
gallery. Her arms were not strong enough to hold her
for long. She fell back to the keg and stood on it, leaning her face against the cool, plastered wall beneath
the window. Tears of frustration started in her eyes.

And then she realized she could hear clearly what
was being said as Mester Bødker tied his horse at the
foot of the stairs.

"Where are my sons?" said Mester Bødker's voice,
so near Helena thought he must be able to hear her
ragged breathing.

"The queen has set them free, Mester. Do not
fear. They are well."

"The queen? You have a queen?"

"Yes, Mester. Bolombo, whom you call Claes, is
our king, and his wife is our queen. This island shall
be their kingdom. They thought to make your sons
servants, respected ones, honored for your sake, because you have healed us many times."

"But my sons have been released, you say. Where
have they gone?"

The two men were mounting the stairs. Helena

could hear the tread of Mester Bødker's boots on the bricks.

"They have gone home, Mester. To Coral Bay. They will be safe. The drums clear a way for them. The drums warn all that Mester Bødker's sons are protected by the king."

Mester Bødker paused on the top step.

"Mange Tak, Asari, thank you," he said simply. "Can you tell me anything of Herre Sødtmann's stepdaughter?"

Helena's heart leaped. She grasped the bars again and pulled herself up, the better to hear Asari's answer.

"I am sorry, Mester," Asari said. "I could do nothing. The little missy is dead."

7

Caroline

Helena slumped on the floor beneath the window, her arms crossed on the top of the keg, her head resting on her folded arms. She was faint with hunger and hopelessness. Mester Bødker had gone, believing she was dead. He had ridden away shortly after Asari took him into the house. He had not been with Bolombo long, surely not long enough to treat the king. Not long enough for Helena to think what to do.

Tears leaked from her closed eyes as she thought of it. Why, oh why had she not cried out to him, signaled him in some way? "They will kill you," Asari had said. Yet how could they hurt her if Mester Bødker was there to save her? "The bussals will surely kill you both," Asari had said. A vision of the blood-slippery table at home rose in Helena's mind. She ground her fists into her eyes to rub it away.

Papa Sødtmann had not saved her, for all he was magistrate of St. Jan and feared by whites and slaves alike. He had not been able even to save himself. Bedstefader Gardelin had not saved her, for all he was the governor. He had gone away to Tappus and had left her behind. Onkel Peder, the soldiers at the vaern, all the other important men on the island had not saved her. They had all, all left her alone to be hurt and starved and marched about the island and locked up forgotten in a storage room.

Helena pounded her fists on the wooden keg and sobbed aloud. No, it would have done no good to call out to Mester Bødker. He cared only for Hans and Peter anyway. She was just a girl. No one thought a girl worth much. And no one cared for her, Helena. They had all gone away and left her. No one cared. No one . . .

No one but Asari.

Helena snuffled and wiped her nose on her sleeve. Asari.

Yes, Asari must care about her, despite the fact he had hurt her. For indeed he had hurt her to save her life. Only Asari had found a way to rescue her from the bloody dining room table.

Helena thought again of Mester Bødker's visit to Bolombo. Why had he gone away so quickly? Was Bolombo perhaps already dead? But Helena had not heard the death wails. Whenever a slave died, the slave women made a frightful racket, and the gombee drums thundered to mark the death.

The Waterlemon Bay camp was silent. Helena

heard litle movement outside. Upstairs in the overseer's house, a muted chanting murmured from time to
time, and a gombee drum beat out a slow, whispering
rhythm, but it was not the rhythm of the dead.

Helena roused herself and crawled to the crates
in the corner. They were fastened securely shut. She
pryed with her fingers until a splinter pierced beneath her fingernail, making it bleed. The tops of the
crates would not budge. If there was food in them, she
could not get to it. And here, in the main house storeroom, she did not even have a trencher of stale water
such as she and the boys had had in the hut. Her lips
were cracked and painful again, and her tongue felt
swollen and parched in her mouth.

She crouched in a corner, trying not to think of
food and drink, and watched the square of light from
the window move across the floor. In the late afternoon, it narrowed again, changing from yellow to gold
to rose.

With evening came the smells of cooking food,
and the hollow in Helena's stomach became a pain. The
band of light from the window had dissolved into
darkness when she heard the bolt on the door shoot
back. She lifted her head from her arms and stared
hard at a sliver of light flickering beneath the door.
Slowly, the door creaked open a crack.

"Missy?" said a whispered voice, and a head appeared around the edge of the door. "Missy 'Lena?
Binne? You inside?"

"Caroline?" Helena held her voice guarded. She
did not know what to think of the Caroline she had

glimpsed from time to time since she was taken captive. The eyes of the new Caroline were unfamiliar to her—not the harmless, docile eyes of the servant who had fanned her to sleep only two nights ago.

"Ya. Ya, Missy. It Caroline. Master Asari send food."

Food. Helena almost wept. She scrambled across the floor toward the light of Caroline's candle, remembering only that it had always been Caroline's task to make her comfortable. She reached eagerly to take the bowl from Caroline's hand.

"Water. Have you water, Caroline?"

"Ya." Caroline thrust a stone water bottle through the crack of the door.

This time Helena remembered to drink slowly. The water, cooled by evaporation in the stone bottle, soothed her lips and tongue. After she had taken several long, deep gulps, she held mouthfuls on her tongue and let them saturate the dry tissues of her mouth and grow warm before she allowed them to trickle down her throat. Then she scooped the gruel from the bowl into her mouth with her fingers until the tasteless stuff was gone.

Eating did not take long. When she settled back to lick her fingers, Helena looked for the first time at Caroline's face, illuminated by the candlelight. The astonishment in the round, glistening eyes took Helena aback. For a moment she wondered what had so surprised the girl. And then it occurred to her that Caroline had never seen her eat except with a silver spoon. I never have eaten with my fingers before, she thought—at least, not since I was a baby like Thomas and knew no better.

"You needn't gape, Caroline," she said sharply. "I was hungry and thirsty. If you had brought me food sooner, I shouldn't have been so starved."

Caroline blinked.

"You lucky Master Asari send you food," she said sullenly.

Deep in Helena's memory, she heard an echo in Papa Sødtmann's voice. "It is their masters who feed them," the remembered voice said. Helena felt her stomach lurch. The gruel sat uneasily, and there was a taste of bile in her mouth.

Caroline was gathering up the bowl and candlestick. The candle's light flickered on her scowling face.

Suddenly Helena felt vastly alone. She did not want Caroline to leave. For, after all, this was her familiar, sulky Caroline, who had served her since they were both little girls. Caroline, with her thin, high-cheeked face, her too-big eyes, and narrow, nervous mouth had always been a part of Helena's life. Helena was used to her. She found herself putting out her hand to touch Caroline's skinny black arm.

"I didn't mean to be sharp, Caroline," she said. "Please don't go away."

Caroline looked down at the grubby white hand on her arm.

"Jeg beder Dem," said Helena. "I beg you."

Caroline put the candle down. She looked at Helena, her face empty and waiting.

Helena left her hand on Caroline's arm. The touch of Caroline's skin was strangely reassuring.

"What has happened, Caroline?" she asked. "I don't understand. Where are all the white people? Why are the bussals keeping me prisoner, and why are you and Asari with them? I don't understand."

Caroline grinned suddenly, and her white teeth gleamed in the candlelight.

"Oh, Missy," she said, crouching on her haunches and rocking slowly backward and forward as she talked. "It the *new* kingdom, Missy! White mans rule *this* island no more. King Bolombo say black mans king of this island. People work for themselves, like in Africa. No more white masters say what to do. No more hunger. No more floggings. No more arms, legs cut off. No more *misery*. That what King Bolombo say . . ." Her voice faltered, and she rocked back and forth faster. "That what King Bolombo say . . ."

"But Asari said Bolombo is wounded."

Caroline rocked faster, moaning a little under her breath.

"Is he going to die?"

Caroline stopped rocking. Abruptly. Something like pain flickered across her narrow face.

"King Bolombo not die!" she growled.

She jumped up, grabbed the candle, and leaned against the heavy door to close it between Helena and herself.

Helena blocked the door with her shoulder.

"Please, Caroline. I didn't mean to make you

angry. Please stay. Please tell me, where are all my people? Why is Mester Bødker the only white person I've seen besides Hans and Peter? And why are they keeping me prisoner?"

Caroline shoved roughly at Helena's shoulder and pushed the door shut. Helena heard her panting as she heaved to the heavy bolt.

"White people gone, Missy," Caroline said through the door. "All dead. When the vaern cannon sound at sunrise two days aback, black people rise up and kill them one time. Only Mester Bødker and his boys spared. And you, Missy. You a slave now, just like me. Queen Lodama's slave."

"Caroline. Caroline!" Helena called. "Don't go, Caroline. Please don't go. You can't mean everyone has been killed. Not my Onkel Peder and Tante Marianne! Not my baby cousin! Not all the soldiers and the Company's men. Not . . . Not . . ."

But Caroline's footsteps had muttered away. Outside, in the darkness, the tree frogs were clamoring their nightly cacophony.

8

The Window

In the storeroom, the passage of time was marked by the window. Helena's second day there began with a faint, rosy lightness high on the wall where the window was. Gradually it grew ruddier as the night insects and frogs ceased their singing. With the first bird's cry came a sliver of scarlet thrown on the wall.

The strange red dawn heralded another day of brooding quiet in the Waterlemon Bay camp. Helena had the feeling the whole island was waiting for something. Now and again the gombee drums muttered, full of foreboding. The day dragged across the floor with the waxing and waning square of light from the window. Helena slept and woke and slept again. She tried not to think. She no longer cried. Crying took too much effort and made her head ache.

After dark Caroline came again with a bowl of food and a bottle of fresh water.

Helena had had to use a corner of the room as a privy, and the place had begun to smell and attract swarms of flies. Embarrassed, Helena showed Caroline the problem. Caroline went away without comment and fetched back a crockery bowl filled with beach sand. She helped Helena dump the sand over the mess in the corner, her nose wrinkling with disgust.

"Use this," she said, handing Helena the bowl.

Helena felt ashamed.

This night, Caroline would not talk, except to turn suddenly as she was leaving and say in a triumphant voice, "I tell Missy, King Bolombo not die! This night Queen Lodama sends once more for Mester Bødker. This night, witch mans let him stay, let him use white man's magic to cure the king."

"Is that why he didn't stay yesterday? Because your witch doctors wouldn't let him treat Bolombo?" Helena was incredulous. "Why, Caroline, they ought to know better than that. All those witch doctors do is a bunch of useless mumbo-jumbo. If Bolombo is badly hurt, he *needs* Mester Bødker."

Caroline drew herself up.

"Witch mans very powerful," she said. "Witch mans make Bolombo well, but the white spirits first must be satisfied. White mans' bullets make holes in Bolombo. White mans' djambis fly into holes, make Bolombo sick. Mester Bødker shall make them come out, witch mans say."

The first two nights in the storeroom, Helena had been so exhausted she had slept deeply despite the hard, chilly floor. The third night, she thought she did not sleep at all. She stared at the place on the wall where the window was, waiting for it to grow light. Her bones ached, but the swelling of her feet had gone down, and she thought she should soon be able to walk again without too much difficulty.

The first sliver of light on the wall was like a gift after the long, dark night. Stiffly, she sat up and pushed her hair out of her eyes. She straightened her gown and took a small mouthful of water from the stone bottle, hoping it would fill for a time the empty place in her stomach. She listened and heard the camp begin to stir to life.

Shortly after dawn Helena heard the hoofbeats of a horse again and Mester Bødker's voice and the ringing of his boots on the bricks of the stairs. And sometime after that the screaming began. Mester Bødker removes the bullets, Helena thought. She tried to stop up her ears, but she could not shut out the screaming, which went on for hours, it seemed to Helena, though the sliver of light had scarcely moved when the screaming stopped.

From time to time, Helena pulled herself up to look out the window. People came and went all morning, mostly women bearing vessels of water and dishes of food up and down the stairs to the house. Helena could smell the food, but none was brought to her. She imagined she would have to wait until after dark again for Caroline to come. She watched for Mester Bødker and planned to call to him if she saw him. He did not appear. She saw a woman leave the house,

her arms full of bloody rags. She heard people talking
quietly among themselves in voices so low she caught
only a word here and there of Danish or slave talk.
When they spoke their African tongues, Helena understood nothing of what they said. But often that day
she caught the name, Bolombo, and once she heard,
"sleeps quiet," and once, "djambis fly away." Finally,
when the sliver of light had grown to a square and
diminished again to a sliver in its journey across the
floor, she heard a jubilant cry.

"Bolombo wakes! The king wakes and asks for
food!"

Helena tried to count the days since she had been
taken from her bed.

There was the day she had been marched to
Waterlemon Bay and put in the hut with Hans and
Peter. That would have been Monday. "Mandag," she
counted, ticking off her thumb.

There was the day the boys were released, and
Asari put her in the storeroom, and Mester Bødker
came the first time. "Tirsdag." She ticked off her
forefinger.

"Onsdag," her middle finger, the day of the red
dawn.

"Torsdag," the day Mester Bødker came back.

"Fredag," the day the bussals held a great obi
celebration, with drums and singing and dancing into
the night and the smells of feasting to torment Helena.
That was the day she caught sight of Mester Bødker
again, and for some reason she did not quite under-

stand did not call out to him as she had planned. And that was the night Caroline had not come with food.

Five fingers and five days.

"Lordag." Helena touched her other thumb. Today was Lordag, Saturday. Today, early in the morning, she had heard the beat of Mester Bødker's horse's hooves and had known he was riding away; her last chance to let him know she lived had gone with him. And today, at last, Asari had come and let her out of the storeroom.

She had been glad to see Asari, but he had spoken to her scarcely at all. He had drawn the bolt, pulled open the door, and said, without stepping into the room, "Come with me."

And she had staggered out obediently and followed him, steadying herself by holding onto the wall, out of the lower story of the house and into the blinding afternoon.

When the light struck Helena's eyes, she stumbled and almost fell. She blinked against the warm radiance and sniffed the air, which, wonderfully, did not smell of herself but of dust and flowers and a salty sea-breeze.

She was outside again. Outside! She wanted to laugh and dance, but the world spun with a faintness that rose from the pit of her stomach, and her right foot still pained when she put weight upon it.

She felt Asari's hand on her shoulder, steadying and guiding her. He walked her a short distance to the kitchen shed and pushed her down onto a bench.

"Wait here," he said, and to the woman bending over the cooking pots, he said, "Give this one to eat."

Now Helena sat on the bench in the sunshine, counting the days on her fingers. Today was Lordag, Saturday, Her belly was stretched and full for the first time in days. She soaked up the warmth and light with her skin.

"Missy, come." It was Caroline's voice.

Helena looked up and saw Caroline standing before her.

"Come," said Caroline impatiently.

"You didn't bring my supper last night," said Helena.

Caroline caught her breath in sharply, and her eyes narrowed.

"I say, come!" she said.

Helena was surprised. Always, when she used to reprimand Caroline, Caroline had been humble and repentent. But since the revolt, Caroline acted differently. She angered easily. She talked back. She was insolent and rude. She gave orders! Orders to her mistress, Helena.

"I will thank you not to speak to me in that tone," said Helena, her full belly giving her courage. "It is not for you to order me about. Much more of such impudence and I'll . . . I'll . . ."

Helena did not like the smirking look on Caroline's face, and she was not prepared for the stinging slap of Caroline's open hand.

"Caroline," she gasped. "How dare you, Caroline!" She held her hand to her reddening cheek.

"Come," said Caroline firmly, and turned on her heel.

Helena looked about her. The woman in the kitchen shed was grinning. A man, leaning against the wall of the house, laughed aloud. Some children, playing in the yard, stopped their running in circles to watch, open-mouthed. All the faces were black or brown. And none appeared friendly to Helena. Her heart began to pound, and the blood rushed to her face. She stumbled to her feet and followed behind Caroline.

9

Slavery

Caroline led Helena down to the beach. She pointed a thin brown finger at the gently breaking ripples of water that lapped the pebbly sand.

"Wash," she said. "You stink."

Helena looked at the cool silver ripples and was suddenly aware of the way her skin itched and prickled. Her hair hung around her face in oily strands. Her hands were grimy. Her gown was smeared with dirt and sweat and dry brown stains. She felt ashamed.

Mama had never allowed her to bathe in the sea. It was unhealthy, Mama said, though Helena had noticed the Minnebeck boys were rarely unwell, and they swam regularly in the bay. Nonetheless, at home, Helena had washed in the plastered stone and mortar tub in the bath house almost every week, and Caroline sponged her with fresh water before bedtime each night. In all her life, she had never been so dirty as she was now.

Helena hesitated, unsure of whether to take off her gown. Some naked brown children were splashing in the shallows a short way down the shore, but no one else was in sight. She stripped off the filthy nightgown and dropped it to the ground. Then she waded out into the water. The salt stung for a moment in the cut on her right foot that was still oozing and inflamed, and the pebbles were sharp, but the delicious coolness of the water far outweighed the discomfort of her hurt foot. It rose about her legs until she was in over her knees. Beyond the coarse pebbles that edged the beach, the sand was soft and smooth and white beneath the green-blue water. Helena sat down and felt the water rise over her body. It was the most wondrful sensation she had ever experienced. The water buoyed her up, so that her body felt weightless. Her arms floated on the surface, light as air. Her feet were lifted by the water, and the surf buffeted her body gently.

Caroline splashed into the water. She had taken off the pink frock. Her skin was smooth and shining where the water glistened it.

"Like this," said Caroline, and scooped up a handful of white sand from the bottom and rubbed it vigorously on Helena's chest. The sand hurt a little, rough against her skin, but when it drifted away to settle on the bottom, Helena could see a clean, pink place on her chest where Caroline had scrubbed, and the skin felt tingly and alive. She scooped up a handful of sand herself and rubbed it on her shoulder; and then she was sanding herself all over and rinsing with the cool water. She dipped her face in and came out sputtering. Caroline's laugh rang out, and then she was laughing herself with the joy of being clean and cool and of moving effortlessly through the water. How could anything so lovely be unhealthy, as Mama had said? It was wonderful. Wonderful!

Helena lay back in the water and felt it rise about her ears and lift her up. Her hair floated out around her face. The sun shone down into her eyes, and she shut them and floated as though in a dream. Caroline floated beside her.

Helena put her feet down, feeling for the bottom, and rubbed at her scalp with her fingers, scouring away the itch. Caroline slapped, flat-palmed, upon the water, and the sparkling drops flew into Helena's face. Caroline was laughing again, her head thrown back, drops of silver glistening on her curly hair.

Helena laughed too, found her footing again, and splashed back at Caroline. Then they were rolling and tumbling in the water like two puppies, splashing in a puddle. For a little while, Helena forgot everything but the warmth of the sun and the coolness of the sea and the answering laughter in Caroline's eyes.

There was to be a council of the leaders, Caroline said. The drums told of their coming, and the women of Bolombo's camp were busy with preparations. From the brush, Helena could hear the frantic squawks of the last scrawny chickens, relentlessly hunted for the cooking pots. Children scrounged for firewood. The plantage buildings were searched once again for food or drink that might have been overlooked.

Lorche found Helena and Caroline behind the cistern at the overseer's house, rinsing themselves with fresh water after their bath in the sea.

"You shiftless gals," Lorche scolded, "don't you waste good water. There scarcely enough for drinking now. And when it rain down, nobody knows." She put her hands on her hips and shook her head, and her voice sounded cross and weary. "You shall put on some clothes and get to work," she said.

Helena didn't say anything. It was strange to be talked to in this way by Lorche, who used to be quiet and humble.

But Caroline sounded as cross as Lorche. "Master Asari say clean Missy," she said. "I do what I told."

"So now *I* tell you, you shall get to work, gal," said Lorche.

"She don't have no clothes," Caroline said, pointing to Helena. Helena was suddenly embarrassed to be standing naked while the two blacks stared at her.

Lorche looked at her critically, and Helena felt small and skinny and very pale before her gaze. She folded her arms across her chest and half-turned away.

"See what can you find in the laundry shed," said Lorche. She shook a finger at Caroline. "Then, gal, you shall get to work!"

Caroline pulled over her head the pink frock she had brought from the beach, then sprinted away in the direction of the laundry shed. The frock's hanging sleeves and undone laces flapped behind her as she ran. That was, after all, her frock, Helena thought; she started to call and then closed her mouth without speaking. Was it her frock now? She didn't know. Everything was upside-down. Lorche was scolding and giving orders. Even Caroline was bossing her. And when she got angry, they only laughed. She could not tell Papa Sødtmann to give them a whipping. But *they* could tell Asari to put her back in the storeroom ... or worse. She waited by the cistern, wishing Caroline would hurry. Even the filthy rag of her nightgown would be better than nothing, she thought, and wondered if she should go back to the beach and search for it.

Caroline brought back a man's cambric shirt. It came only to Helena's knees, and the sleeves were much too long, but it was almost clean and light and marvelously cool. Helena thought she must look funny, with her pale legs sticking out beneath the voluminous shirt. She cast another glance at Caroline in the pink lawn frock. It was none too clean, for Caroline had been wearing it for days and dark stains spread beneath the sleeves. Even unlaced, the frock fitted closely and was hot and uncomfortable, Helena knew. She decided, for the time being, Caroline was welcome to it.

Her hair was a problem. Helena had never dressed her own hair. That was Caroline's job. But suddenly Helena did not dare ask her to do it. She tried to comb it with her fingers, envying the way Caroline had only to shake her head to arrange her

tight black curls. Caroline stood, hands on hips, waiting for Helena. The hair was an impossible task. It
was long and heavy and hopelessly snarled. Helena
felt tears of frustration well in her eyes.

There was a hand on her shoulder.

"Sit, Missy," said Caroline.

Helena sat down on the ground, and Caroline
knelt beside her and, with gentle fingers, worked the
snarls out of the long, light brown hair. She tied it at
the nape of Helena's neck with a strip of cloth, torn
from Helena's too-long sleeve. Helena didn't know
what to think. Why did Caroline help her? Was it
habit? Or was it something else?

"Mange Tak, Caroline," she said, almost whispering.

When Lorche thrust a twig broom into Helena's
hands and indicated the jumble of broken furniture
and other ruined household goods that littered the
gallery, Helena did not demur. She and Caroline set
to the task of clearing the place where the council
was to be held.

As they hauled armloads of rubbish down the
steps and around to the back of the house, Caroline told
Helena about the bussal leaders.

"Bolombo king," said Caroline. "But Prince
Aquashi and Kanta also great mans. Kanta help capture the fort from the soldier mans. Kanta fight at
Duurloo's plantage with the king the first day. Aquashi
lead the attack up the island. Together, them three
plan it all."

Helena was tugging at the end of a small, carved

cupboard, whose splintered doors swung loose on their hinges. Caroline pushed at the other end. They were beginning to perspire in the late afternoon heat.

"Who made Bolombo king?" Helena said, panting. "I mean, I know he was called King Claes by his owner, but I thought that was a kind of joke. We have . . . we had a field slave called Prince, and so does . . . did the Company. I thought . . ."

The cupboard tipped over the railless edge of the gallery. It fell with a crash, disintegrating into a heap of broken boards on the ground. But at least the gallery was cleared. Caroline turned away from the edge and wiped her hands on her pink petticoat.

"Bolombo not *made* king," she said firmly. "He *born* king—first-born son of Adampe king's number one wife—in Africa. Bolombo only king on St. Jan, but there many, many noblemans on this island from many tribes: Adampe, Aquambo, Amina."

Helena nodded, trying to sort the names into some kind of sense.

"Now," Caroline said, indicating the broom that leaned against the wall. "Now, you sweep."

Jarred from her thoughts by Caroline's peremptory tone, Helena felt a flash of anger.

"What are *you* going to do?" she said.

Caroline glared.

"Missy sweep," she repeated.

Helena grabbed the broom and took a few angry, awkward swipes at the gallery floor. This was ridiculous, she thought. She *had* been helping, after all. Caroline had no right to be so bossy.

"I teach Missy *how* to sweep," Caroline said, her voice husky with laughter, and Helena looked up to see her grinning. "You, Missy, don't know nothing," she said.

Gently, Caroline took the broom from Helena's hands and began to sweep with firm, even strokes.

"Like this," she said, and Helena stood, looking on, still not knowing what to think.

10

Moving Camp

"Adampe. Aquambo. Amina." Helena tested the unfamiliar names on her tongue. "What tribe do you belong to, Caroline?" she asked when they had finished and were sitting in the shade, surveying the cleanly swept gallery.

Caroline shrugged.

"Don't know," she said. "I born on St. Thomas. I never live in Africa."

"But didn't your mother and father come from Africa? I was born on St. Thomas too, and so was my mama, but I still know I'm Danish. Denmark is where my grandparents were born."

"Don't know my mother," said Caroline. "Don't think I got a father. Maybe old Master. Maybe not. Don't know."

Helena was silent, shocked. Not to know who

your mother was, or your father! How very strange! She herself couldn't remember her own father, but she knew who he was—Andreas Hissing, a bookkeeper of the Company, who died of fever when she was small. She glanced at Caroline, who had leaned her head back and closed her eyes.

Why, Helena suddenly wondered, had it never occurred to her before to ask about Caroline's parents? She had assumed they were among the other Sødt-mann slaves. Slaves didn't seem to stay together in families. Perhaps, as Mama had said, they didn't care about each other the way white people did. There was so much she didn't know about Caroline, she thought. She had never really talked to her before, except to give her orders, of course. And yet, Caroline was quite pleasant to talk to—actually quite as pleasant as a Danish girl might be.

A great bonfire had been built from the remnants of the broken cabinet and other ruined furniture in the open space before the gallery. From her vantage point behind the queen, Helena could see the faces of the gathered bussal warriors in the ruddy glow of the flames.

Bolombo had been carried out of the house upon his pallet and propped against cushions at the head of the gallery stairs. Helena thought he looked ill, his face grayed and tight about the mouth, his eyes sunken back beneath his brows; but he held his head as proudly as he had the day she first saw him on the

road, commanding his people. Behind him were
ranged his retainers, heavily armed, and Asari squatted at his right hand.

The two visitors flanked him. Their retainers, also
carrying guns and knives, crowded close to the foot of
the gallery. Helena thought the visitors didn't look
very friendly. She leaned forward, trying to catch the
meaning of what they said.

Lorche nudged her, and Helena sighed. She had
been given the task of fanning the queen, but she kept
forgetting. She started once again to move her arm as
Caroline had showed her, back and forth slowly and
steadily. Slowly and steadily. The fan was a leaden
weight that made her arm ache.

The man they called Prince Aquashi had risen to
his feet. The others fell silent, and Helena sensed a
tense expectancy in the air. Aquashi glowered sullenly, his eyes ranging over the gathered warriors,
his black brows bristling in a way that reminded
Helena of Papa Sødtmann. In fact, Helena thought,
and was startled by the thought, Prince Aquashi re-
sembled Papa Sødtmann in more ways than one: he
was short and stocky, with a high-domed forehead
and heavy jaw; he had an air of ponderous impor-
tance, and a cruel, heavy-lipped mouth.

Helena could not understand his African tongue
when Aquashi began to speak, but she heard the anger
in his voice. As he spoke, the warriors muttered, scowling at one another and at Bolombo. One of Aquashi's
followers brandished his flintlock. Helena's fan arm

slowed once more, but Lorche didn't notice. She too was leaning forward, tense and listening.

Helena saw Asari help Bolombo to sit straighter. Bolombo seemed to gather himself together; his chin went up proudly, and he did not deign to look at Aquashi as he answered. His eyes swept the faces of the assembled warriors, and his voice, firm and commanding, quieted their grumbling.

Aquashi retorted heatedly, his heavy lip twisting.

Beads of sweat gleamed on Bolombo's forehead, touched crimson by the light of the fire. He spoke with authority.

Now the other leader, Kanta, jumped to his feet. He was shouting, gesturing with one muscle-corded arm, and Helena noticed the other arm was held stiffly against his naked chest beneath a dirty bandage that swathed his shoulder.

When Kanta had finished speaking, Bolombo leaned back against Asari's arm and closed his eyes for a moment. His voice, when he replied, sounded weaker and suddenly tired. He spoke slowly and clearly, as though to little children, but still Helena could not understand the strange-sounding African words.

Bolombo fell silent and looked at Aquashi, and Helena thought his eyes bored into the stocky black man; but Aquashi did not flinch. He glared back.

Kanta had taken a step toward the king, and Bolombo's men shoved forward protectively. Kanta was trembling, and his eyes looked wild to Helena.

Bolombo held up a hand and spoke again.

Among the warriors, there was a rustling sound, like a breeze through dry pods of women's tongue trees. Kanta and Aquashi looked at one another, and Aquashi nodded. Slowly, they sat down. Bolombo leaned back and closed his eyes.

In front of Helena, the queen shifted and muttered to the fierce black woman at her side. Helena remembered her task and began to wave the fan again. Back and forth, back and forth, the fan pulled at Helena's aching arms. She squeezed shut her eyes, which burned with the leaping of the flames.

Whatever the leaders had argued about, Bolombo seemed to have won, Helena thought. He truly was a king, whether born or made.

The voices of the bussals murmured around her, and the fire hissed and popped as a board shifted and broke with a crash. With her eyes closed, the voices sounded like a meeting of the planters in Papa Sødtmann's study. In those meetings, Papa Sødtmann's will had always prevailed. Helena felt glad Prince Aquashi had submitted to Bolombo. She opened her eyes and concentrated on moving her arm back and forth, back and forth, as she fanned the queen.

Helena and Mester Bødker's family were not the only white people left alive on St. Jan. As the days went by, Helena became sure of it. She heard talk of the vaern being retaken by a force of loyal slaves and knew, when she heard it, the slaves must have been commanded by whites. Two days after the council, Bolombo suddenly moved his camp. They were fleeing soldiers, Caroline said as they were loaded with bundles of food and cooking implements and marched up the steep path toward Herre Frøling's holding on the hill to the north.

Helena's foot was still sore, and as she limped and perspired under the heavy burden she had been given to carry, she wondered what soldiers Caroline could mean. The soldiers at the vaern were dead, or so the bussals said. Perhaps these were soldiers sent over from St. Thomas by Bedstefader Gardelin. Perhaps they had been sent to rescue her. At the top of the hill, Helena dropped gasping and exhausted to the ground beneath a newly planted genip tree. The spindly little thing threw only a small patch of shade, but it was planted in a spot that afforded a view of the bay below. Helena hoped she might see the soldiers if they came and perhaps attract their attention. She nursed her foot and waited for the hilltop breeze to cool her reddened face and quiet the pounding in her head while the bussals milled about the abandoned Frøling plantage buildings.

Helena squinted her eyes against the glare of blue sky and bluer water, hoping every minute to see soldiers trooping over the road toward Waterlemon Bay. She began to imagine what it would be like when the soldiers took her back to her mother—how Mama's blue eyes would widen in surprise and then fill with tears of joy, how she would hug Helena and kiss her and whisper how sorry she was she had left her behind. Helena was so lost in her dream that Caroline's urgent tugging at her arm startled her. The bussals were forming a ragged procession behind King Bolombo's litter.

"Missy. Missy, 'Lena," Caroline was saying. "Come. Make haste."

Helena cast another look down at the bay road. There was no sign of movement anywhere.

"I'm coming, Caroline. Don't pull at me so!" she said irritably.

Helena limped away from the little genip tree. Her foot was hurting dreadfully now. She hoped they did not find too good a hiding place. She wished the soldiers would come at once. The tears started in her eyes, and she brushed them away and snuffled noisily. It was bad enough the way the pounding sun made her head ache when she walked, without adding tears. She emptied her mind of thoughts of Mama and Mama's pretty blue eyes and concentrated on putting one foot before the other on the rocky trail.

She and Caroline caught up to the procession following King Bolombo's litter. From then on, Helena scarcely noticed which way they went. It was away from the soldiers. Of that she was hopelessly sure.

Camp was made at last at Madame van Stell's small summer house on the point above Brown's Bay. Helena had been here when she visisted her Onkel Peder's plantage on the bay below. Madam van Stell's was some distance from the wagon trail that skirted

the point. The paths approaching it were steep and
overgrown with brush.

As servants of the queen, Helena and Caroline
were assigned sleeping places on the side gallery,
beneath the window of the room where the queen
installed herself. The stone floor of the gallery was
cold and hard, but by now, Helena found she could
sleep anywhere she was allowed to lie down. She was
always tired and often hungry. She fell asleep whenever she was left in peace for a few moments, and she
had begun to understand what she used to think was
the "laziness" of slaves.

Helena still felt a seething kind of anger when
she was given orders. She was made to gather firewood
and to haul water from the hogsheads beneath the
monkey pod gutters of the roofs. Since she had not
been allowed to bathe again, the splashes of water she
spilled as she carried the buckets made muddy streaks
on her dusty legs and feet.

There were not so many people in this camp as
there had been at Waterlemon Bay. Kanta and Prince
Aquashi had taken their followers to other camps, and
some warriors had been left behind at Frøling's plantage. Also, a few of the women and children simply
slipped away and did not come back.

The second night in King Bolombo's new camp,
the women wailed their cries of death. There had been
another battle between Bolombo's warriors and the
soldiers, Helena learned. Some of the bussals had been
killed. The wife of a dead warrior moaned and rocked

her body to and fro, her face smeared with dust and her eyes white and staring. Helena watched, fascinated. Mama said blacks did not care for one another as white people did, yet the woman seemed genuinely distraught. Helena wondered if Mama had been so grieved when Helena's father died.

11

Hunger

Helena opened her eyes. In the blackness overhead, stars pricked with silver thread a pattern in the sky. Helena turned, trying to find a comfortable position on the pallet of plantain leaves Lorche had shown her how to make. She wondered if she would ever be used to waking in the night to the light of stars and moon, instead of the comforting darkness of a strongly shuttered room. Already she could hardly remember how her soft bed had felt. At least, she thought, here on the gallery a pleasant breeze stirred the hot night air to waft mosquitoes away.

Helena heard voices in Queen Lodama's room. Perhaps it was the voices that had awakened her. She closed her eyes and tried to go back to sleep, but the voices kept nudging her awake. It was the voice of Breffu, the knife-wielding warrior woman, that

brought her wide awake, eyes open, ears straining
to hear.

"I say, kill the missy!" said Breffu's voice. "She
do half a child's work, or less. She a danger. If the
masters know Bolombo holds a white child, they try
to get her back."

"The masters know not Bolombo holds her," said
Queen Lodama. "They think she dead."

Helena hugged herself for comfort. She thought
about what Lodama was saying. It was true. Bedstefader was not looking for her. He was not sending
soldiers to rescue her. Mester Bødker would have told
him she was dead, of course. Everyone thought her
dead: Bedstefader, Mama, Onkel Tham and Onkel
Willum, Onkel Peder and Tante Marianne . . . if *they*
lived . . . Helena bit her lip. What a fool I was to not
cry out to Mester Bødker, she thought. He *might* have
found a way to save me. At least he could have let
them knew I am alive. But, in her heart, she knew
she had not been wrong. They would have killed her
if she had cried out, and they might kill her yet. At
least they did not harm Mester Bødker. It was small
comfort. Her throat ached and her ears ached as she
listened to the low voices of Breffu and the queen.

"These mans here," Breffu was saying now,
"these mans no good to us also. They good for talk—
much, much talk—and drinking rum and sleeping all
the day. They good for fighting among themselves—
who gets biggest plantage? Most servants? Highest
rank? Mans always like this. Talk, talk, talk and

drink much rum. And still this island belong not to whites, not to blacks. And womans got no shelter. And children cry for food."

"It the way of mans," Lodama said gently. "In Africa, mans fight for glory or loot or womans and go home to rest when weary. Here fighting different—not a game. Here fighting not stop because warriors weary, but our mans know this not. They learn. Soon King Bolombo strong once more. Soon Asari gets powder and lead for our muskets. Soon the warriors fight . . . and win."

Helena had pulled herself up to kneel beside the window. Cautiously, she peeked into the room. Lodama was sitting cross-legged against the far wall. A small cresset lamp illuminated her face, glinting dully on the iron hoops that swung from her ears, picking out the delicate tracery of scarified designs that curved across her cheeks. Lodama's face was still. She seemed at ease, her hands resting quietly on bare thighs. But somehow, Helena thought, struck by a look in Lodama's eyes, she looked worried. Her serenity was not real, Helena decided, and did not know how she knew it.

Breffu's stocky form blocked Helena's view of the queen from time to time. Breffu paced, ranting in a voice forced low. Her head was sunk between her brawny shoulders, and her fists were clenched at her sides.

"*Now* the time to fight!" Breffu said. "Now while the masters got no help from other nations. We not safe 'til every master die or go away forever. We must hold this island *now*. It death for us all if they take it from us. Death!"

Breffu's voice made Helena's mouth go dry. Her legs trembled, and she sank down onto her pallet again. She did not want to see Breffu's face.

"Death!" Breffu was crying, her voice hoarse and filled with hate. "Already we begin to die. I say, kill the missy to pay for our dead!"

Helena put her hands over her ears. She wanted to run, and she knew she could not. Bolombo's guards were posted everywhere. Beyond them was the forest— a dark and death-filled place for one who did not know it.

From inside the room, Helena heard sobbing, despite her covered ears. The sound of Breffu's pacing footsteps had ceased. Soft and soothing, Lodama's voice crooned above Breffu's angry weeping, as though she sang a fretful child to sleep.

Helena had found a blackened yam, overlooked by the cooks, in the cold ashes of last night's fire. She glanced about to make certain no one saw her, and then she slipped it into a fold of her shirt.

She was so hungry her stomach rumbled at the thought of how the yam would taste. Perhaps, though burnt, its center would still be good. If she could find a solitary corner, she might be able to eat it before someone snatched it away. She moved out of the cook shed quietly, hoping no one would notice and call her to a task.

Helena edged past the group of women who squatted, talking, in the shade of the summer house. She heard the sound of voices from the laundry shed where some of the women were washing clothes in spite of Lodama's orders that water be used only to drink. All her life, Helena had heard black slaves called dirty. It made her wonder at the way they strove to keep clean, even in defiance of their queen.

There was no sound from the stable. Part of its roof had fallen in, and Helena did not think the bussals were using it. Perhaps she could escape curious eyes there. She held the yam against her body beneath her arm and ambled toward the stable, expecting every moment to hear the familiar, "Missy, you shall come." But no one spoke to her, or even seemed to notice her progress across the yard.

At the stable door, Helena stopped and looked back over her shoulder. No one was watching. She slipped through the doorway into the ramshackle building with a sigh of relief.

A pool of sunlight puddled the floor beneath the opening in the roof. The corners were deeply shadowed, but Helena could see no one was there. The two stalls, where Madame van Stell had stabled her cart horse and her mule, had been torn down, like every other movable piece of wood on the place, and carried away for firewood. The stable was empty, except for the fallen-in roof thatch and some broken harnessing heaped in a corner.

Helena squatted, unable to wait another minute, and took out the yam. She broke it apart. Inside the crisp black skin and dried outer meat, there was indeed a golden center, still soft and sweet. Helena stuffed a piece into her mouth greedily.

A baby's wail made her freeze, her hand halfway to her mouth with another chunk of yam. She ceased chewing and held her breath.

It was a thin, fretful wail, more like the weak cries of a newborn kitten than those of a child. It came from outside, behind the stable.

Moving her jaws soundlessly, Helena chewed and swallowed her mouthful of yam. She tucked the rest beneath some wisps of moldy straw gathered near the door and crept back out of the stable, not making a sound. Cautiously, she advanced along the side of the building until she could see around the corner. The baby and its mother were just behind the stable, out of view of the yard. The mother sat slumped against the stable wall, her legs sprawled out before her. She was intent on the baby lying on her arm.

"Ya, ya," the mother crooned. "Ju sa trik, lille. Yes, you shall drink."

She guided her breast to the baby's mewling mouth. He took the nipple and suckled and then turned his head and began to whimper again, the dry nipple slipping from his lips. The mother sighed and tried to get him to take it again.

"Ju sa trik, lille," the mother coaxed, and Helena heard something helpless, and hopeless, in her voice.

Helena could see that the woman's breasts were dry, empty and withered and flat. Helena knew the look of milk-plump breasts—the round brown breasts of slave mothers kept so long in the fields away from their little ones that they dripped milky fluid, and her own mother's breasts, blue-veined creamy white and rich with milk for baby Thomas. She wondered why the mother kept urging the baby to drink when there was so obviously nothing for him to drink because . . . because she is hungry too, Helena thought. She has no milk because she has not had enough to eat herself.

The taste of yam in Helena's mouth soured suddenly. She watched the baby turn his head from side to side, his mouth seeking and rejecting the empty breast again and again. He beat tiny, pink-palmed hands against his mother's shriveled breast, and Helena saw how thin his arms and legs were, how distended his belly.

Poor lille, Helena thought. Poor hungry little one. She remembered how fat her brother Thomas was, and how loudly he howled if his dinner was late. Poor lille, Helena thought.

The yam would do him no good. A single burnt, half-eaten yam could not bring back his mother's milk. Helena thought she could smell the yam, though it was inside the stable, under the straw. His mother needs lots of food, Helena thought. A yam is not enough.

She looked at the baby again. His tiny face looked old. Wrinkles like worry lines puckered his forehead. His mouth sucked air.

Helena crept back around the stable to the door, went inside and took out the hidden yam. She squatted, looking at it, and brushed off wisps of straw and specks of dirt. Turning it over in her hands, she smelled its scent, and her mouth watered. There is only enough for me, she thought, and she broke off a tiny chunk and let it melt slowly on her tongue. The taste of it made her stomach roll.

Then she jumped up and ran out of the stable, back around to where the mother sat. She dropped, almost threw, the yam into the startled woman's lap.

"Take this, you," Helena said and caught a glimpse of surprised eyes turned up to her as she whirled and ran. She got as far as the summer house steps before she burst into tears.

12

The Storm

The men had the drums to bring them news. Bolombo knew everything that happened on the island, every move Prince Aquashi and Kanta made. It was likely the other rebel leaders knew as much about him, for the drums told when Bolombo sent out his trusted lieutenants to put the people to work planting cotton and new cane rattoons. The drums beat out messages about fighting in Coral Bay and about treacheries, both white and black.

Caroline told Helena what the drums said. There was war between the rebel leaders now. The Amina, Kanta, had run amok. He burned the plantages Bolombo wished to preserve for the kingdom.

Bolombo sat on Madame van Stell's gallery, still weak from his wounds, and his face was like thunder at the news the drums told. Helena watched him from a distance and knew it did not go well with the rebellion. At Bolombo's side, Asari looked grave, his face drawn thin.

Perhaps now, when they are fighting each other, Helena thought, the soldiers will come, and I will be saved.

Helena saw that news passed among the women in a different way. It passed in whispers, like a breeze that blew from camp to camp with the wandering of the rootless women. The men did not seem to notice the way the women came and went. There were always women to cook and do what work needed doing, and the men seemed to not care that the faces continually changed. The women traveled from camp to camp, seeking husbands, lovers, children. They looked for food and water and shelter. They looked for a place to belong. And wherever the women moved, their news moved with them, almost as swiftly as the messages of the drums. But the women's news was not of desertions or trading or battle. It was of where food might be found, or shelter, or perhaps a lost child. And now it was of death. The old had begun to die, the old and the very young. In Bolombo's camp, a baby whose mother had no milk for him ceased to breathe in his mother's arms, and the women's whispers told of it, though it was beneath the notice of the drums.

The queen, Lodama, did not wander. She and Breffu and the Adampe princess, Suplica, remained with the king for almost a month. And with them were their servants: Lorche and Caroline and Martha and

Helena. Helena watched as Lodama listened to the whispers. Calm, unmoved, she heard all there was to tell about the condition of the people. Breffu raged and harangued the king until he turned his back and would listen no more. Suplica complained, her voice loud and querulous. But Lodama just listened and watched and waited.

The storm began in the night with a pattering of raindrops bouncing and rolling in the dust. The drops rustled in the dry leaves of the trees and tapped hollowly at the wooden shingles of the van Stell summer house.

Helena heard the sound and woke and, for a moment, did not know what it was. The shower swept across the house and yard so quickly it was over by the time she realized it was rain. She lay on her pallet, staring into a night blackened by heavy clouds, and sniffed the freshened air. She pulled her legs up inside the warmth of her shirt, wrapped her arms around her knees against the new coolness and closed her eyes.

When she woke again, it was to water driven roaring against her face. The rain writhed in sheets across the gallery, hurled beneath the gallery roof by gusts of violent wind.

She struggled to her knees and tried to see into the night. The black rain slashed against her squinted eyes. Her ears were full of the shrieking of the wind and the heavy thunder of rain on the gallery floor. Arms, thin and wet, clutched at her, and she knew by their feel they were Caroline's. She pulled Caroline beside her, against the wall, and they clung together, deafened and blinded by the storm.

"Inside," Helena screamed into Caroline's ear. She felt the word being torn from her lips and smothered in the wet and dark. She knew Caroline could not hear her. Groping her way along the wall toward the place where she knew there was a door, she pulled Caroline along behind her and knew from the willing way Caroline came, that she had the same thought. They must get inside.

The door was beneath her hand. Helena fumbled at its surface, searching for the handle, and it gave way suddenly from under her, thrown open by the force of the wind and, she realized a moment later, by the release of the inside bolt. Helena stumbled into the passage, and Caroline fell through the doorway on top of her. Water was running in a stream across the floor. They could feel its flow around them. Then warm hands were lifting, pulling them out of the way, and the door was forced shut again.

Helena was on her hands and knees. The roar of the storm was muffled now as the thick door closed. The air inside the passage felt empty and cold against her wet skin. She shook her head, trying to clear her face of the dripping weight of her hair. The passage was dark, and she could see nothing, but a voice comforted the darkness, urging her and Caroline to their feet and guiding them on.

The room into which Helena stumbled was relatively dry and quiet after the maelstrom on the gallery. She and Caroline were led into a corner, away from the windows. The floor was wet beneath their feet, but furniture and wooden crates had been stacked against the wall. The girls were pulled and lifted onto them. Helena still held fast to Caroline's hand. She gasped for breath. The driving rain had filled her nose and mouth. Now she sputtered and coughed as though she had been drowning. As her coughing subsided, her teeth began to chatter, and she felt Caroline's thin, wet fingers trembling in hers.

Someone was stripping off her sopping shirt and rubbing her with a rough dry cloth. She let go Caroline's hand, conscious that Caroline was also being rubbed dry. Helena's skin began to tingle warm again.

"Mange Tak," she said over and over to the warming hands. "Mange Tak. Many thanks."

She was beginning to distinguish shapes in the darkness, and to hear voices. There were people in the room, many people, squatting on the boxes piled against the wall. The woman who was drying her was a tall, ample shape, blacker than the dark. Helena could smell her pleasant, earthy warmth.

"Come, sit by here," the woman said, and pulled Helena down into the circle of her arms. Helena recognized the gentleness of that voice. She could feel in the strength of the warm, encircling arms the solid tranquillity of Lodama, the queen.

The storm lasted through the night. From time to time, Helena woke, startled by thumps and crashes that sounded over the steady roar of the rain. Some-

time after dawn, she woke and could not sleep again.
Lodama's arms were still around her. The queen
seemed not to have slept. Her broad, brown face broke
into a gleaming smile when Helena looked up at her.
She helped Helena to sit up and rubbed her arms and
legs again to make them warm. Helena did not know
what to think. The queen was not treating her like a
servant at all. She was so kind.

"Mange Tak," said Helena, but somehow "thank
you" was not enough. She knelt before Lodama and
chafed the queen's chilly feet and hands. Lodama
chuckled and said something Helena did not understand, and the people around them laughed.

Caroline slept on, undisturbed by the laughter,
Helena saw, her head in Martha's lap.

It was impossible to tell what time it was. The
day dragged on, the wind lessening as the hours
passed, the rain pouring steadily, a gray veil before
their windows. When the veil began to thin and, at
last, diminished to a fine mist, it seemed as though
they had been crouched on the crates for days, numbed
to paralysis by the storm. Slowly, the people began to
stretch cramped limbs, to sigh, to groan, to climb from
the crates and head, stumbling, across the flooded floor
to the door. Rushing water gurgled in the monkey pod
gutters. Helena could hear the splashing cascade into
the hogsheads beneath them. They would not need to
conserve water for a while.

When the queen stirred, Helena jumped from
their crate and put up a hand to help her down. The

queen took the hand and landed, lightly and gracefully for so big a woman, beside Helena, splashing in
the water on the floor. She inclined her head.

"Mange Tak, 'Lena," she said, in her heavily
accented Danish. She walked away, across the room,
speaking to the other people in an encouraging tone.

Helena stood looking after her, confused at her
own feelings. The queen had been kind to her, had
comforted her during the storm, had held her while
she slept. The queen had said thank you in return for
courtesy, had said it respectfully in Helena's own
language. But she had called Helena " 'Lena." Not
"Missy 'Lena" as a respectful slave would do. In
former times, that would have gotten her a flogging,
Helena thought.

Helena's heart pounded with the renewed realiza-
tion of her changed station. Lodama is not *my* slave,
she thought. I am *hers.* And suddenly Helena realized
it had been a long time since she had called the queen
by her slave name, Judicia, even in her thoughts. It
can mean so much, what a person is called, Helena
thought. Perhaps that is why we give slaves new
names when we buy them. Their African names be-
longed to them when they were free. When we give
them new names, we make them ours. We make them
feel like slaves. That was what had struck home to
Helena when Lodama called her " 'Lena." So long as
black people called her "Missy 'Lena," she felt like a
mistress. But just plain " 'Lena" made her *feel* like
a slave.

Musing, Helena sloshed across the room, down the passage, and out the open door onto the gallery.

The sun moved from behind a cloud just as Helena came out the door. It struck the water dripping from the roofs and trees and standing in puddles in the hollows of the yard and turned the wet world to silver. Almost immediately, wisps of mist began to rise from the ground. The sun felt good on Helena's face. The cloth Lodama had wrapped sarong-fashion around her was damp, and her hair was still wet. She felt the sun suck the moisture from her water-soaked body, and she closed her eyes against its brightness and luxuriated in its warmth.

Then she opened her eyes and looked across the yard. The bussals were wandering, dazed-faced, through the muck, stooping now and again to retrieve a pot or a basket or some other item that had been blown from its place. The roof of the cook shed was gone. The stable had collapsed to the ground. The little garden plot Breffu had caused them to plant behind the laundry shed was a silver lake. The sprouting vegetables they had planted—the young tania and chick peas and calelu vines—had been washed away. Everywhere Helena looked she saw devastation: trees uprooted, branches flung like kindling sticks.

"Ai-yeee!" she heard Lorche wail from the ruined cook shed. "Ai-yee! Ai-yee!" Lorche rocked from heel to toe and tore her hair and mourned, as though death had come once again to Bolombo's camp. The few remaining baskets of grain had overturned, the grain was scattered, soaked, upon the ground. There had been little to eat before the storm. Helena wondered if now there was anything at all.

13

The Trail

"The people must live," Queen Lodama said. "Dead folk cannot taste freedom in *this* land."

The king gazed out toward the English island of Tortola from his vantage point on the north gallery of the summer house. He ignored his wife, who knelt respectfully before him.

"If children die, if mothers die, the people dead forever," Lodama said. "St. Jan not like Africa, where new womans may be taken from other tribes."

Helena wondered why the queen had called the women to the gallery to hear her speak to the king. And why did he pretend they were not there? He stared out to sea, past Lodama's head, and his eyes did not flicker as she spoke. It was as if none of them existed, Helena thought—not the queen, who knelt before him, speaking in her low, clear voice, or Breffu, who stood to one side, her face dark and passionate, or the women, who had gathered to hear. Why did Lodama try to advise the king, Helena wondered. Men never listened to women. Had Papa Sødtmann ever attended to Mama's hesitant suggestions?

A child whimpered, and his mother hushed him.

Suddenly Bolombo spoke, not to Lodama, but to Asari who sat, as usual, by his side.

"Prince Aquashi got many womans," Bolombo said. "Kanta also. A king may find in this kingdom many womans who make no trouble. Many fertile womans who live through famine times."

Asari held his thin face expressionless and said nothing. Bolombo frowned at him.

Helena was watching Asari's face. Sometimes it seemed to her she must have dreamed the day at Waterlemon Bay when Asari told her it was he who saved her life. He had not spoken to her since, except to bark an order now and again. He seemed to have forgotten who she was. Does he care about me at all, Helena wondered. Does anyone care about me? Caroline? Lorche? The queen? Why *did* Queen Lodama hold me safe and warm all through the storm two nights ago?

"The womans of Prince Aquashi leave his camp," Lodama said. "The womans of Kanta leave his camp also."

For the first time, the king's eyes moved in response to her words. He was surprised, Helena realized from the odd look on his face. He hadn't known. His drums and runners hadn't told him what the women had known for days: that gradually, most of the rebel women on St. Jan had left their men and gathered together in a camp of their own on the high flatlands between Bourdeaux Mountain and Amina Hill.

Lodama's voice had taken on the chanting quality of a ceremonial pronouncement. "I, Lodama, the queen, and Breffu, the first noblewoman of Bolombo's kingdom, go also," she said. "We go to make a place of shelter for the mothers and the children." She put her hand on the gleaming curve of her abdomen. "We carry the life of the people within us," she said.

Helena looked at Lodama curiously and knew suddenly what she was saying. The queen's middle was growing thicker, despite the scarcity of food. She's going to have a baby, Helena thought.

"Warriors must eat to fight," said Bolombo sullenly. It was the first time he had spoken directly to his wife.

"Ya," said Lodama. "Where there not food enough, warriors must eat first. But womans also must live. That why the womans make a camp. It time to live apart."

Breffu's voice rasped suddenly, interrupting Lodama's conciliatory words. "It time warriors fight masters, not each other," Breffu said.

Bolombo turned on her, his face blazing. "Kanta burns the plantages," he shouted. "Aquashi plots against the king."

"Then kill them!" screamed Breffu. "Kill the warriors of Aquashi and the warriors of Kanta who should be your allies. Put your own warriors into battle with them and let them kill their brothers. When warriors weak, the masters finish you. But Breffu done with quarrels and with waiting. For womans, white masters or black all the same. Still people starve! Still children die!" She whirled and stomped from the gallery, shoving her way through the handful of astonished women.

Lodama bowed her head to the gallery floor.

"The warrior heart of Breffu weary," she said quietly. "The mother heart of Lodama also."

She rose when Bolombo did not reply and looked deeply at his sullen face. He avoided her eyes.

"We leave before day," she said, and motioned the women to follow her.

Beside Helena, Caroline was giggling nervously. "Tell him good," she said.

Helena was impressed. She tried to imagine what would have happened if ever Mama had spoken to Papa Sødtmann as resolutely as Lodama, as defiantly as Breffu.

A month of going barefoot had toughened Helena's feet. The walking was easier this time. If she were not so hungry, Helena thought, she might feel strong indeed. She was proud to find how easily she could keep up with the others.

Queen Lodama had put her and Caroline in charge of the little children. There were four, three boys and a tiny black sliver of a girl. Helena picked her way down the steep path from the point, holding the little girl's hand. When the child stumbled and fell, Helena lifted her up and was amazed at the fragile lightness of her body. Caroline showed Helena how to sit down to let the little girl climb onto her back to cling around her neck. She was not *very* heavy, Helena thought. There was something in her solemn eyes and the serious way she sucked at her thumb that went to Helena's heart.

Fortunately it was early, the dawn still gray. As soon as the sun came fully up, Helena knew the forest would begin to steam. The path was still deep in mud. It sucked at Helena's feet, but felt cool and smooth.

The path came out on the main wagon trail near her Onkel Peder's plantage. Helena cast a glance at the deserted buildings. Shutters had blown off the estate house windows in the storm, and the clearing was littered with branches and debris, but the heap of bloody rags at the foot of the stairs had been removed. Helena wondered again about her uncle and aunt. I should ask what became of them, Helena thought. Someone would know. Why don't I ask? But she never talked to the bussals about her own people. She liked to think everyone was safe on St. Thomas. I don't want to know, she realized as she looked back for one more glimpse of Onkel Peder's house.

Helena trudged along, shifting the position of the child on her back from time to time. The little girl was silent and inert. Caroline herded the boys in front of them. One had sore eyes, caked with drying matter that attracted the tiny stinging gnats. The gnats did not seem to bother him, for he did not lift his hand to wave them away, but he stumbled often over rocks and roots, and Helena thought he could not see well.

The sun rose in the sky, and with it, moisture rose from the drying forest. Soon the air was thick with damp, and Helena's shirt was wet and clinging; the breeze that touched her overheated skin felt briefly cool, but not cool enough to bring relief.

The wagon trail climbed steeply over the ridge and steeply down again past the terraced, weed-grown fields of Judge Hendrichsen and Herre Suhm. Helena could see the blue of Coral Bay from the top of the ridge. They would pass her house on their way, Helena knew. Her heart pounded to think of it.

At the grigri tree near Suhm's, they rested. The cisterns at Suhm's were as full of water as those at the summer house. They drank their fill. The little girl fell asleep, her arms wrapped around Helena's neck.

From Suhm's, the walking was easy, the road wide and paved with flat cobblestones and blocks of cut sea coral. Already weeds sprang between the stones, encouraged by the recent rain and the month-long cessation of wagon traffic. Brown doves minced ahead of them on the road, flying up with cooing complaints when they drew near. Helena woke her small burden and made her walk. The going might be harder later on.

They passed Mester Bødker's house without stopping. There was no sign of life there or on Vaern Hill. Helena knew the exact place in the road where she would be able to see her own house. It was hard to lift her eyes to look.

The house had a vacant, staring look. Its loose-shuttered windows were like eyes, horror-struck. The gallery and yard were as littered with debris as every house they had passed. Helena hoped someone would clean it up before Mama came back again.

"In this place, we rest and eat," Lodama said.

The women were climbing to the gallery. Helena put her foot on the bottom step and could go no farther. Bedstefader's hammock flapped, shredded in the breeze and torn from its hook at one end.

Caroline urged Helena to come up to the shaded gallery, but Helena shook her head stubbornly and sat down on the steps. The little girl sat down beside her and sucked her thumb; her eyes did not leave Helena's face.

The women were peering into the windows cautiously. Lodama walked through the big door into the passageway. Breffu, on the gallery, divided and passed out small portions of moldy bread, salvaged from the storm. Caroline brought a chunk to Helena, and Helena broke off tiny pieces and fed them to the little girl. The bread stuck at the lump in her own throat, and after one attempt to swallow it, she did not eat any more herself.

They left the road at Helena's house and crept through the thicket of brush that edged the shore. The children had been sternly ordered to be silent, and even the babies seemed to understand and obeyed.

Near the warehouses, Breffu left them waiting while she scouted ahead. Helena searched around the warehouse yards with her eyes and recoiled when she recognized what hung from the spreading branches of the Company's great grigri tree. She stared, mezmerized by the gleam of white bones turning in the breeze.

When Breffu signaled all was clear, they ran, crouching, across the clearing in front of the warehouses, past the tree and its gruesome fruit, and into the brush again. Out of sight of the Company buildings at last, the Company windmill only a toy tower on a distant hill, they dropped down, panting, to rest. Helena wondered why they had passed the Company holdings so cautiously, but she did not ask. I am learning, she thought ruefully, to do what I am told without question.

The little girl crawled into Helena's lap and put her ear against Helena's heart. Caroline and the little boys sprawled close by.

When she had her breath, Caroline grinned. "Got you a child, I see," she said, pointing to the little girl.

Helena looked down at the dusty little head pressed to her breast. "Where is her mother?"

Caroline shrugged. "Gone," she said.

With the tail of her shirt, Helena wiped the little girl's sweaty face and then straightened the rag she wore for a frock. When she put her cheek against the woolly top of the child's head, the child stirred and sighed, then turned up her face and clamped her arms around Helena's neck.

14

Lille

The journey to the women's camp at Kob Flat took two days, with many stops for rest. The women followed the wagon trail around Coral Bay as far as the deserted de Cooning plantage the first day. They camped that night, fireless and hungry except for the last of the bread they carried with them.

Once in the night, Helena woke terrified. Something was moving in the brush outside the house where they had taken shelter. She lay paralyzed for long moments, her heart huge and thumping in her chest, before she realized it was only the clatter of hermit crabs, clumsy in their borrowed shells, scrabbling against rocks and fallen branches. When at last she could make herself move, she snuggled closer to the little girl who had curled at her side. She concentrated on the sound of the little girl's breathing and the feel of it against her arm, gentle and warm—alive.

They moved at dawn, and by the time the sun was fully risen, they had reached the tiny, rocky beach south of Sabbat Point. Lodama and Breffu walked away from the women to the water's edge and stood talking, the water lapping at their toes. Helena sat down on a boulder to watch them, wishing there was something to eat. Some of the children were crying. The little black girl was scratching her head, digging skinny fingers into her woolly hair, and whimpering. It was the first time Helena had heard her make a sound. She pulled the child between her knees and inspected her scalp. The little girl's hair crawled with lice. The skin of Helena's own scalp prickled at the sight.

"Ugh," she said. "Come, lille. Come, little one, you need a bath."

She stripped the child's ragged garment off, shrugged off her own shirt and, carrying the child, picked her way across the rocks to the water.

Beneath the lapping wavelets, treacherous clumps of purple-black sea urchins softly stirred thin, sharp spines in the moving surf. Helena could see an area clear of rocks and urchins some distance out. The sandy patch of bottom looked invitingly clean and white beneath the clear blue water. Gingerly, Helena threaded a passage between the threatening spines, the water rising cool and refreshing about her dusty legs. When she reached the sandy place, the water was thigh deep. She set the little girl down and was startled to find the child clamoring up her legs, crying out in terror.

Helena crouched down and tried to reassure her. "It is fun, lille," she said. "See, it is fun."

She held the little girl steady with one hand and scooped handfuls of water up to trickle over the child's chest and back. The little girl whimpered, but Helena kept smiling and talking to her gently. Soon the little girl quieted. She looked at Helena with huge, uncertain eyes and clung to her arm, but she did not struggle against the water. Helena knelt on the sandy bottom and scrubbed the little girl with sand as Caroline had taught her. Wherever she scrubbed, the child's skin turned a beautiful, rosy brown. Helena washed her face, cleaning her encrusted nose, careful not to splash the salty water into her eyes. She laughed to see the little girl lick her lips again and again to taste the salt.

Little by little, she coaxed the little girl to lie back in the water until her curly wool was wet. Helena scrubbed at the little girl's scalp with her fingers and rinsed her hair over and over. The little girl closed her eyes and floated in the circle of Helena's arms and finally, for the first time, Helena thought she saw her smile.

"You a good little mother, 'Lena," said Queen Lodama's voice, very near.

Helena started. She had been so absorbed in bathing her charge, she had forgotten the others.

"Oh," said Helena. "Is it time to move on?"

"First we eat." Lodama's smile flashed, white and wide, at the hopeful look on Helena's face. She held out a dripping hand, creamy palm up. On it were some shells shaped like small, lumpy cornucopias.

Some sort of sea snail, Helena thought, her nose wrinkling doubtfully.

"Bring your child, little mother," Lodama said, laughing now. "You see. A hungry belly finds many things good."

The snails—Lodama called them "whelks"—*were* good. Helena and the little girl squatted with the other children and the women around a fire that had been built on the beach. The sunshine dried them, prickly with salt, but clean. They sucked the meats out of the hot shells as fast as Lorche could dip them from her pot. The only trouble with whelks, Helena thought, was they were so small and few. Her stomach still grumbled when the pot was empty, but Breffu said there was no time to gather more from the rocks. When some of the women protested, the queen made a sudden, deep clicking sound with her tongue, and the women fell silent and began to gather their bundles and straggle after Breffu, who headed purposefully inland through the low thorn bushes and treelike cacti.

Quickly, Helena shrugged into her shirt and dropped the little girl's garment over her head. "Come, lille," she said and took her hand.

The little girl looked up trustingly and smiled again, a small, shy smile.

As they walked, Helena thought.

"Does she have a name, this little one?" she called to Caroline, who trudged ahead of her, the sore-eyed boy on her back.

Caroline shrugged. "That one Missy 'Lena's child now, I think," she said, grinning over her shoulder. "It for Missy to call her name."

"What shall I call you, lille?" Helena said.

The little girl put her thumb in her mouth and looked at Helena with round, cocoa-colored eyes.

"Lille," Helena mused. "Surely you are a lille, a little one. Why not 'Lille'? Do you like that name? Shall I call you 'Lille'?"

The little girl was stumbling, churning her scrawny legs to keep up with Helena's longer steps. She held tight to Helena's hand and darted wondering looks at Helena's questioning face.

"Lille," Helena said, bending to sweep the little girl into her arms. "From now on, that is your name."

Lille sighed and lay her damp head in the curve of Helena's neck. She sucked her thumb and closed her eyes.

The women had chosen a good place, Helena thought.

She did not even see the huts until, climbing around a sharp bend in the steep trail, suddenly she was among them. They huddled, twenty or so palm-thatched dwellings of various sizes, on a relatively flat bench of land at the head of the ravine up which the travelers had been climbing. Behind the huts rose a steep cliff, festooned with vines and ferns. It was a sheltered, hidden spot, canopied with shade-casting lignum vitae trees. "A safe place," Caroline said.

It was also, Helena learned, a place where food and water were, if not plentiful, at least available. Because of the recent storm, clear fresh water seeped from the cliff to gather in a pool at its foot and run down the ravine—or "gut," as the women called it— in a narrow, rushing stream. But even when the rain water dried up, there were cisterns at nearby deserted plantages to supply the women's needs. It was the gardens of these remote plantages that had first attracted them to this place. The gardens furnished a fairly steady supply of millet and tania and yams for the women who camped in the gut.

Sometimes Helena wondered who had ruled the camp before Queen Lodama and Breffu arrived. The people at the camp greeted them as though they were awaited and showed them where to sleep. Then they gathered around and waited for the queen to tell them what to do.

Indeed, perhaps the people *had* been waiting for a leader. Helena saw that many of the huts were in sorry repair. Refuse seemed to have been tossed everywhere, and the children used the stream in the gut for a privy. The bigger, younger women were sleek and strong, but some of the old and sick seemed near to starving.

Helena was surprised to see there were men among the people. Most were old or very young, boy-men. But in the evenings, warriors drifted into the camp to visit with their families. The men acted differently in the women's camp. They came and went quietly, making no demands. The women seemed content for it to be so.

Breffu was the one who began to organize the camp. She set some of the people to repairing the broken huts and others to sweeping them out and clearing the ground around the dwellings. She directed the children to gather the garbage and carry it to a place where the land fell steeply away from the trail. Shouting with laughter, the children threw the garbage over the edge, to fall, crashing through the dense foliage, to a place out of sight and smell below.

Breffu chose a place for the privies—behind large boulders deep in the undergrowth a short distance from camp. She sent out foraging parties to hunt stray animals and to gather fruit and to dig edible roots. She sent others to tend the plantage gardens. She taught the little children how to capture lizards and birds in small snares and showed them where birds' nests filled with eggs were likely to be. She set the oldest women to watching the babies and assigned certain women, under Lorche's direction, to cook at communal fires. She posted guards, both day and night, at the top of the cliff and some distance down the trail and worked out a system of signals that sounded to Helena astonishingly like the calls of forest birds. Morning and night, she called the women together to eat, and she saw that the food was divided fairly. All her orders were given after consultation with Queen

Lodama, and always she said, "Queen Lodama say, you shall do this."

In Bolombo's camp, Lodama and Breffu and the Adampe princess, Suplica, had ruled the women. In the women's camp, Lodama and Breffu continued to rule, but Suplica's authority receded before the powerful personality of Café.

Café had arrived at the camp before them. Caroline said she was the favorite of Prince Aquashi, and Helena wondered about her reasons for leaving him.

Café stood almost a head taller than even Lodama, but she, unlike Lodama, was as slender as a silver palm. Her skin was the color of her name, coffee rich with cream. Her hair hung to her waist, straight and shining as a blackbird's wing. That was the Spanish in her, Caroline said, that straight, long hair. Café was from Hispaniola, bought off a passing ship to wet-nurse the van Bewerhoudt babies. But it was hard for Helena to imagine her a nurse for children. Café smouldered, it seemed to Helena, sullen and irritable and savage-tongued. The women scurried when Café spoke. The children kept away from the sound of her voice. Suplica faded to querulous subservience and, within a week, deserted back to Bolombo's camp.

But strangely, Helena noticed, Breffu seemed drawn to the half-Spanish woman. For long hours they talked together, one voice kindling the other. Breffu would squat on her powerful haunches, her gleaming black skin a startling contrast to Café's creamy limbs.

At night, when warriors visited the camp, and the women sat, swaying, around the fire to clap their hands and sing while the men drummed and danced, Breffu would blaze with joy, it seemed to Helena, to see Café leap suddenly into the firelight, a flame herself, and begin to dance with the men.

15

The Field

"You and you and you shall go to the millet field today," Breffu said one morning when they had been in the women's camp about a week.

Caroline nudged Helena, who was feeding thick gruel to Lille by scraping it from the pot with her finger and holding out her finger to the little girl to suck.

"Me and you, Missy," Caroline said. "Breffu say, me and you."

Helena looked, astonished, after Breffu's rapidly striding figure. "Me?" she said.

"Ya, and me." Caroline got up and kicked at the hard-packed ground with her bare heel. "I no field slave," Caroline said. "Don't know what make her send me to go."

"You?" said Helena. "What about me?"

Caroline grinned a wicked grin. "We both come

down in the world, Missy," she said. "That the truth. We both come down."

"You starve, you down, gal," said Lorche with a groan as she struggled to her feet, rubbing her back where it ached from bending over the cooking pot. "Field work some up from that."

The other women and girls were rising from their places beside the morning cooking fire. Early sunlight began to dapple the ground. In groups of two or three, the women straggled away to their morning tasks.

Lille sucked noisily at Helena's finger.

"What should I do with Lille?" Helena asked.

"Leave her with the old womans," said Lorche. "They mind her while you gone."

But Lille would not stay with the old women. She opened her mouth in a pearl-studded pink howl when Helena tried to leave her. She clamped her scrawny arms around Helena's legs and hung on for all she was worth, and her keening screams tore at the morning air and silenced even the birds. In the end, Helena took her along.

They marched to their destination single-file. Caroline carried a hoe over her shoulder, and so did the woman Breffu had assigned to the millet field, but Helena had only a grubbing stick. Lille trotted cheerfully behind, her face unmarked by her recent tantrum. She did not let Helena out of her sight.

The millet field lay near a ramshackle house that must have been used once by an overseer. The field had been cleared of rocks, the rocks piled into a wall that bordered the field on all sides. The recent rains had irrigated a flourishing tangle of weeds and grass. Caroline and Helena paused at the wall and looked at the overgrown field helplessly.

"I no field slave," Caroline muttered again. "Don't know this work."

The woman climbed over the wall of rocks, using her hoe like a walking stick to steady herself. Helena got a good look at her for the first time that morning, for she had been so occupied with Lille that the woman had been far ahead on the path before she was able to follow.

"Why, you're one of *our* people," Helena said. "Aba, isn't it? I'm certain you're our Aba!"

Aba's yellowed eyes seemed to look straight through Helena. She grunted, then headed for the far end of the field, her voice coming back at Helena on the morning breeze. "I Aba," she said. "Not Devil Sødtmann's Aba no more."

As she walked away from them, Aba stripped off her ragged frock and tossed it on the wall. Helena looked at the retreating woman's naked back. The shining smoothness of the skin was marred by puckered stripes of pink, where a whip had cut. Aba bent and began to hack the soil with her hoe, and the scarred flesh rippled over her smoothly moving muscles. Her breasts hung down and swung in time to the motion of the hoe.

Her eyes on the cruel scars, Helena swallowed hard. She felt her face grow red.

Caroline's eyes flickered to Helena's face. Helena turned away, bending to lift Liile over the wall. When

Caroline began to scramble over the wall, Helena followed her.

Caroline and Helena took turns with the hoe and the grubbing stick, trying to imitate the seemingly effortless labor of Aba. Aba moved along the field, her hoe rising and falling steadily, and behind her a straight line of moist, black earth, deeply cut and webbed with roots of weeds, appeared as if by magic. The furrow the girls made was, by contrast, shallow and wavering. Sometimes it took both of them, working with stick and hoe, to break through the strong weed roots. Helena found herself trampling over newly turned ground, packing the soil down again with her feet, undoing their work as fast as it was done. Her hair came loose. Her sweat dripped in her eyes and her shirt clung wet to her back. Between her shoulders, a pain began to knife, and the stick chafed her palms.

"Let us stop to rest," she panted, halfway down the field.

Caroline was willing, but when they laid down their tools, Aba frowned and came striding to them.

"At midday, you stop to eat and rest," she said.

The pain was scarlet behind Helena's eyes. "I will rest now," she said. "*Now*, do you hear?"

Aba lifted her hoe threateningly. "You shall *work* now," she said.

"Nej." Helena turned her back and walked toward the shadow of the wall, where Lille sat playing with a little pile of sticks.

"*Breffu* say, Missy *shall* work," said Aba.

Helena felt a lurching in her chest at the sound of that name, spoken with quiet menace. Over the pounding of her temples, she could hear in memory the voice of Breffu, quivering with violence. "She do half a child's work," the voice had said. "I say, kill the missy!"

The ground swam crazily before Helena's eyes. The hand she put out to steady herself met only air. She saw Caroline come up to her, holding out the hoe. Caroline's eyes were wide and afraid.

"Come, Missy," Caroline said.

Helena did not look at Aba. She walked with dragging steps to the place where they had stopped, lifted the hoe, which felt leaden in her hands, and swung it at the earth.

By late afternoon, Helena's anger had congealed to hate. All her body was an agonizing pain, wet with sweat and grimy. Against Caroline's advice, she had taken off her shirt and worked naked as Aba did in an attempt to cool herself. Each time she swung the hoe, she thought she could not possibly lift it up again. Yet time and time again she did lift it and chop at the unyielding soil, until the rhythm of the hoeing was part of her pain and part of her hate. She had long since ceased to see. The heat glared wavering from the ground and the salty sweat in her eyes blinded her. She and Caroline worked side by side, and Caroline moaned, low under her breath, but Helena clamped her lips shut and would not make a sound.

"*Thwack!*" went the hoe, and Helena imagined it was Aba's body it struck. "*Thwack!*" and she imagined the hoe biting into Breffu's black flesh.

"*Thwack*" and "*thwack*" and "*thwack*," the hoe cut the earth, several times after Aba said, "Enough for this day." It was Caroline's hand on her arm that finally stopped her. The hoe slithered from Helena's numb fingers, and she sank to the ground where she was, the pain of stopping almost as great as that of going on.

Aba had headed home to camp, and still Helena and Caroline slumped on the ground, too tired even to crawl to the shade. It was a tiny voice, saying her name, that made Helena open her eyes.

" 'Lena, 'Lena," the voice whimpered.

Helena struggled up on one elbow and shaded her eyes against the slanting rays of the sun with her other hand. A small black figure, haloed in red by the setting sun, struggled across the field, dragging something with it. Helena blinked and squinted. It was Lille, stumbling over the clods of broken earth. She dragged a water skin and called, over and over, " 'Lena. 'Lena."

Caroline stirred and sat up painfully. Helena pushed against the ground until she too sat, swaying. She held out both hands, as Lille staggered the last few steps, and took the skin from the little girl. She pulled out the stopper with fingers stiff and bloody from the hoe and hefted the bag to her lips. The water gurgled out, warm and sweet, onto her face, and she gulped it and let it run over her chin and chest in a soothing stream.

Lille plopped herself down beside Helena's knee. Her forehead was wrinkled, and her eyes were dark wells of worry. She patted Helena's leg with one dry little hand.

Helena lowered the water skin and passed it to Caroline, who was reaching out eagerly to take it.

"Lille, you said my name!" Helena realized. "You clever child, you talked. You said my name." She hugged Lille hard and found herself laughing with a strength born of Lille's water and of her caring.

The first days in the millet field were much alike. They passed in a shimmer of heat and pain, broken only at middays by short rests in the shade and long drinks of water and little food. At days' end, Helena and Caroline had barely strength enough to drag themselves back along the path to camp.

After the first day, Helena wore her shirt no matter how hot she was. The fever of her sunburned back and buttocks, the product of her first day's foolishness, made the nights a haze of pain and sickness, as well as the days. She dreamed, over and over again, of what she had seen on the dining room table the day of the revolt, and she dreamed of being flayed and burned alive. Yet between the dreams, she sometimes came to a consciousness of a cool hand on her forehead and of something soothing being gently spread on her quivering flesh.

In the daytimes, it was her anger that kept her going—anger at Breffu and Aba, anger at the rebels for tearing her world asunder, anger at Papa Sødtmann for allowing them to, even anger at Mama and Asari for their differing desertions. She cursed under her breath as she worked, using words she had heard the sailors in the harbor say. But she did not cry and she did not, as she thought she surely would, fall dead from fatigue.

Indeed there came a day when she awoke from a dreamless sleep and felt refreshed and ravenously hungry. The ache of her body was only a faint undercurrent to her movements. The bloody blisters on her palms had calloused, hard and dry. The sunburnt skin of her back had peeled to reveal a painless layer whose golden tan matched her arms and legs. She felt . . . Strong, Helena thought. How strong I am!

That day she noticed she and Caroline were almost keeping up with Aba. Their furrows were as clean and deep, almost as deep, as Aba's furrows were. Helena came to the end of her last row just as Lille trotted over to show her a bit of speckled eggshell she had found beneath a tree. Helena glanced at the shell and smiled and looked back across the field, which was broken and weeded and ready for seed. She felt not only strong, but proud. "Half a child's work," indeed! Helena thought. She wished Breffu could see the field. She ruffled Lille's woolly hair and was startled to hear Aba grunt, as she strolled past, a low, reluctant, "Good."

16

Bo Akutia

Lille rolled, giggling, in the dust with the sore-eyed little boy.

Helena sank down beside Caroline to watch while she ate a handful of inkberries. "Want some?" she asked, extending her open hand to Caroline.

Caroline did not even look up to see what was offered. She slumped, her arms resting loosely on her bent knees, her head held dejectedly in her hands. "Nej," she muttered.

The children were up and chasing one another around the huts. Lille was smaller than the sore-eyed boy, but his dim vision matched him fairly equally with the shortness of her legs. When he stumbled, Lille caught up to him and, shrieking, tagged him. Then they changed places, and he chased her.

"They are full of good spirits," Helena said.

Caroline sighed, a deep, hopeless sigh that seemed to come from her belly. "Babies don't know nothing," she grunted, and the words lost themselves beneath her hands.

Helena cocked her head and stared at Caroline. She chewed reflectively on an inkberry seed. "What troubles you, Caroline?" she said.

Caroline shifted, shrugging one shoulder irritably.

"Caroline? Do you feel sickly?"

Caroline lifted her head. She turned her great, dark eyes on Helena. They were dull with pain. "Nej," she said. "Not sick."

"Then what?"

Caroline searched for the words. They came out haltingly and low, and she looked at the ground again as she spoke. "Weary," Caroline said. "I weary and . . . ya, maybe I sick . . . here . . ." She put her hand on her chest. "I got bad feeling here . . . Not body pain, but inside . . . my heart weary and sore."

Helena nodded and did not know what to say.

"Before time, they say . . . they say the new kingdom coming," said Caroline. "They say no more slaves, but I still a slave. They say people work for themselves, but I work for the queen and Breffu. They say all get food and houses and fine clothes . . . and no more misery . . ."

She raised her head, and Helena saw her look at the straggling, palm-thatched huts, the bare foot-beaten ground between them, the cooking fire and coal pots where Lorche and her cook-women hovered with spoons in their hands. Daylight was fading. The setting sun threw washes of orange light across the faces of the women who squatted, resting, in front of the huts. It picked out the shadows beneath their eyes and the lines around their mouths. Except for the cook-women, no one spoke. They stared into space, or closed their eyes, and listened to the bird sounds diminish as the hilarity of the children increased. An old man moved in front of the fire with a lurching, sidewise gait, hitching along a leg that was shriveled and stiff. Helena thought she understood. The women's camp looked a poor, struggling place, and the people looked worn and sick.

"Too long," said Caroline. "It go on too long. By and by, I think, the masters come back."

Helena scooted closer to Caroline and laid a hand on her knee. "I will take care of you, Caroline," she said. "When it is over, I will tell them how you helped me. I will keep you with me always and take care of you, and I will not let them sell you. I promise."

Caroline looked at Helena again. The light had faded so Helena could not see her eyes, but she could feel them on her. There was a long silence while Helena felt the uncomfortable power of Caroline's eyes. Then Caroline sighed again, and there was such sorrow in the sigh that Helena's heart squeezed painful in her chest.

"Mange tak, Missy," said Caroline.

It nagged at Helena when she thought of it later that she had heard no gratitude in Caroline's voice. Only resignation . . . and hopelessness.

. . .

It was Prince Aquashi who came first of the leaders to the women's camp. "Come like a moth to Café's fire." Lorche chuckled. His swagger did not fool her, or anyone, Helena thought.

Helena thought Breffu would be sorry to see Aquashi. But Breffu greeted him almost as though she expected him and gave up her place beside Café to sit on the other side of the fire.

If Helena was surprised to see Prince Aquashi in the women's camp, the arrival of King Bolombo a few evenings later truly astonished her. She and Caroline were picking lice from Queen Lodama's hair when, beneath Helena's exploring fingers, she felt the queen grow still. Nearby, Lorche ceased grinding millet and hunched, as though frozen, over her grinding stones. Lille and the other children left off their games to stare. The gossiping women fell silent. The men, wagering at bones, suspended their play.

Helena looked in the direction she saw their eyes move and saw King Bolombo at the edge of the clearing, surrounded by warriors abristle with muskets. He did not move until all the camp was quiet. Then he strode to the open place before the fire.

Aquashi came stooping out of the doorway of Café's hut and straightened to look Bolombo in the eye. They glared at one another while the silence in the camp drew taut. Then Aquashi reached to scratch his belly, yawned elaborately, and turned his back.

Quickly, Lodama stood with a fluid motion that

belied the growing swell of her pregnancy. She moved to stand before her husband and bowed.

"The king welcome in the womans' camp," she said. "Come, rest by the fire. Eat and take ease. In this camp, people not fight," Lodama said. "Here all brothers and sisters leave their quarreling."

That first time, Bolombo was gone again by morning; but three night later, he came back, with only Asari and Cotje, unarmed, to accompany him. And this time, he behaved in an extraordinary way.

Aquashi and his lieutenants had been lounging near Café's hut, drinking rum and boasting of battles, when Bolombo appeared. They fell silent a moment. Then, suddenly, Aquashi began to laugh as though he did not see the king. He began to tell a story of chasing an enemy into the sea until water filled the enemy's mouth. "He throw away his knife," Aquashi bragged, "and vomit seawater at my feet." Nervously, Aquashi's men laughed with him and also pretended the king was not there.

Helena was watching from the shadows of Lodama's hut where she had carried the sleeping Lille to lay her on their pallet. She saw King Bolombo saunter to the center of the camp, where all could see him, and gesture to Asari. She saw Asari go to him, and kneel, his head touching the ground at Bolombo's feet.

When Aquashi's voice was running down, searching for words to keep the silence at bay, suddenly

Bolombo spoke, and Helena was reminded of the first time she had heard his voice, on the Konge Vej. There was a power in Bolombo's voice that made the listener tremble. It was a kingly voice, Helena thought, a voice of dignity and command. But now Bolombo was saying the most unlikely things. He was shouting angrily, and his anger was directed at Asari's bowed head.

"Traitor to the people!" the king shouted. "You bring quarrels to the kingdom, when all should band together. You mock the true-born king!"

Helena was bewildered. Asari was Bolombo's most trusted lieutenant. What could he have done to earn the anger of the king? Why did he cower, unprotesting before the king's abuse, stripped of dignity before all the women's camp, and especially before Prince Aquashi?

"You not fit to serve the kingdom," Bolombo was ranting. "Your treachery wounds the heart of the king."

Asari fell face forward in the dirt. He did not lift his head.

Helena peered out at the faces of the watching people. All were looking, not at King Bolombo and Asari, but at Aquashi who, throughout the tirade, was staring stony-faced over the heads of his men. Bolombo's voice rose louder and louder. His face twisted in rage as the words poured from his month.

Bolombo grabbed a handful of Asari's long, straight hair. He lifted Asari's head and dealt him a ringing slap across the face. Then he let go Asari's hair and turned sharply on his heel. Cotje followed him into the forest.

Asari lay unmoving in the dust. Still, Helena saw, no one looked at him. All eyes followed Aquashi as he slowly rose and disappeared into Café's hut.

It was as though the whole camp sighed at once. First there was a murmur, then a giggle, and then, all through the camp, people were laughing and calling to one another as in a festival. Amazed, Helena crawled from the doorway. All about her, the people were repeating the same words.

"Bo akutia," they said. "Bo akutia."

Asari rose from the ground and brushed the dust from his arms and legs. He was smiling, Helena saw.

"It is the custom, Missy," Asari told Helena next day. He had been conferring with Lodama and, as he left her hut, stopped suddenly to speak to the girls, as though on impulse.

"When one man is offended by another," Asari said, "his anger may make his spirit sick. The anger must be vented. But if the man abuses his offender, the offender must take offense, and the quarrel will go on without end. Bo akutia rids both of bad feelings.

"The king says to me, his friend, what he feels against Prince Aquashi. I, being his friend, take no offense, for I know the words are not meant for me. And Aquashi, because the anger has rained on *my* head, also cannot take offense. The king is rid of his anger, and no new anger has been made. Now, in time,

perhaps the king and the prince may come to be
friends again. Bo akutia. A way to end a quarrel."

Asari squatted before them, smiling his gentle
smile. "You seem well, Missy," Asari said. He looked
her up and down. "Well and strong," he said.

"I am," Helena said, and realized with surprise
that she was.

Asari himself was very thin, Helena thought. His
eyes had a shadowed, sorrowing look. Helena opened
her mouth to reproach him for ignoring her so long
and then closed it again. I cannot stay vexed with him,
she thought, when he seems so sad. She smiled back.

"And you, Caroline?" Asari was saying.

"Work too hard," Caroline grumbled, "but we
gets enough to eat by here."

"Do you still serve the queen?"

"We work in the fields or gather food most days,"
said Helena. "The queen stays here in camp where
there are others to see to her. But we sleep in her hut."

He nodded seriously, considering her answer. "I
am glad to see you well, Missy. There may be a time
when it will be good to remember Queen Lodama
spared your life and showed you kindness." His eyes
caught Helena's and held them. "Will you remember,
Missy, if ever a time comes when the queen needs
your help?"

"What do you mean? How could *I* help *her*?"

"*Will* you remember?" Asari said, and Helena,
impaled on his gaze, nodded yes.

17

Trust

It soon became commonplace for Aquashi or Bolombo, or both, to visit the women's camp. Of the rebel leaders, only Kanta stayed away, though his woman, Bomboe, joined the women.

Every evening, the people gathered at the council fire, built high against the darkness. They sang, and more and more often, against all tribal rules, Café rose to dance the dances of war.

Lodama said such a thing never would have been in Africa. "But this war belong to womans also," Lodama said. "This not like Africa, where mans war alone for glory and loot. Here all the people make war and all dance—for victory over the white mans, for making the people free."

Waking one morning in the queen's hut to the feared and hated sound of Breffu's voice, Helena learned Bolombo and Aquashi were allies once again.

"Soon, soon an end to this comes," Breffu exulted.

Helena saw Lodama's smile flash in the dimness of the hut.

"With the warriors united, we drive the masters forever from this land," Breffu said. "We strike and kill the devil masters!"

Over Breffu's shoulder, the queen caught Helena's eye. She nodded her head almost imperceptibly toward the doorway. Obediently, Helena untangled herself from the sleeping Lille and crept silently to the door. There she scrambled into the warmth, away from the hoarse, exalted voice of Breffu, saying like an incantation the words, "Strike! Kill! Strike! Kill!"

When the rebellion was two months old, Kanta came at last to the women's camp. It was the news of the Great War Dance, drummed from ridge to ridge along the length of the island, that brought him. But he said he came to visit his woman, Bomboe.

"Even fierce ol' Kanta not want to miss this dance." Caroline giggled.

Helena wondered if this was Breffu's plan. One by one, it seemed, she and Café had lured the leaders together. Bit by bit, they were forging the warriors into a single force, enflamed by battle songs and dances of war.

Every day more men arrived at the women's camp, and the women slaved to provide food and drink sufficient for their growing numbers. Breffu was everywhere at once, it seemed to Helena, who tried to avoid her. Breffu's ringing voice transformed the camp to bustling purpose, to excitement and hope.

There were some, however, who did not like the change. Over her cooking pots, Lorche grumbled. "Them lazy mans lay about up to no good," she said. "Sleep in the daytimes. Drink rum all the night. Eat all the food!"

"They forget this camp belongs to the womans," van Bewerhoudt's Alma, worn thin from nursing her sickly baby, said. "They like masters: 'Do this thing! Do that!' Don't lift no hand to help."

"Work getting harder," Caroline said. "I more better off before time."

It was Caroline who told Helena about the army of planters gathering at the vaern in Coral Bay. "They sure to fight soon," Caroline said. "Who win, think you?"

Helena's heart was thumping. "Soldiers?" she said. "A large force of soldiers with cannon and muskets?"

Caroline nodded.

"The rebels have muskets, but not much powder," Helena said. "Some have died, and some have deserted."

"Not all shall fight," said Caroline. "Some people wait to see what passes."

Helena knew Caroline was right. The accustomed slaves were less likely to fight than the bussals. It was the accustomed slave women she heard grumbling now. The arrival of the men had not relieved their weariness or their helplessness. Once again they had become servants, now to their men.

"Leastwise, before time, I eat my own cooking," Lorche said. "Leastwise, before time, I don't feed no layabout mans."

Helena and Caroline were scrubbing Lorche's cooking pots with soapy maran leaves.

"Before time, I don't scrub no pots," Caroline said glumly as Lorche muttered away toward her hut to rest.

Helena looked down at her hands. They were rough and brown, the ragged nails grimy. "No more did I," she agreed, knowing Caroline was referring to the time before the rebellion.

She thought of what Mama would have said to see such ugly hands. Mama had made her wear mitts when she went out in the sun, to keep her hands white. "A lady is known by her hands," Mama used to say.

". . . Mester Bødker . . ." Caroline was saying.

Helena focused her mind again.

"What did you say about Mester Bødker?"

"Kanta say he with the soldier mans in Coral Bay."

Helena looked hard at Caroline. She searched the sad brown eyes and considered the discontented mouth.

"White masters strong," Caroline said, shaking her head. "By and by, I think, masters win."

"I think so too, Caroline," Helena said, an idea forming in her mind. "Please don't worry. I will take care of you no matter what happens."

Caroline looked sidewise at her. "Ya," she said. "There no new kingdom. That a dream. Reckon, do I got to be a slave, I just as soon belong to Missy."

Even *she* knows we were better off before the rebellion, Helena thought. She thought of all the time since then, of playing together in the sea and working together in the millet field. She remembered the night of the storm and the feel of Caroline's arms around her neck. I can trust her, Helena thought.

Helena took a deep breath and hesitated. Then, "If we could get to Coral Bay," she said in a rush, "Mester Bødker would rescue us."

It had all happened so fast, Helena's head spun a little to think of it. One day it was just Caroline and she, idly wondering if they dared to slip away from the women's camp to find Mester Bødker at Coral Bay. The next thing she knew, there were six of them, if one included Lille—and I could not leave her behind, Helena thought—and the plans for escape were fixed.

They had had to confide in Lorche.

"We cannot go alone," Caroline pointed out. "We don't know the forest paths."

"I studying to go home," Lorche said. "Reckon now Master Sødtmann dead, our Missy 'Gitta a tolerable mistress. But I tell myself, how the masters know a faithful slave from a rebel? Black look black to white folk."

"I will tell them," Helena said, though in her heart, she herself questioned Lorche's trustworthiness. The memory of Lorche's wicked grin beneath the brim of Mama's blue-ribboned hat was still too clear. But still she said, "I will tell Mester Bødker you helped me. He is a fair man and will not let them punish you. And I am certain Mama will be kind to you for my sake." She paused, and something made her add, cunningly, "Perhaps she will reward you."

Lorche pursed her lips thoughtfully and gazed at Helena through narrowed eyes. "If Missy swear we faithful, reckon we get no flogging," she said. "I go."

But Lorche did not know the way either.

"Path we come by too long," said Lorche, "and it follow the bayside where we cannot hide. People do say there another way, 'round Bourdeaux Mountain. Maybe Alma knows."

Alma did know an overland route to Coral Bay. Since her baby had died a few days before, Alma was dejected and bitter. "Go or stay no matter," Alma said.

Anniche, Alma's pretty cousin, squatted at her side as the women talked. She said, "Come, Alma, let us go with the missy. I weary of this place."

"Can we trust her, think you?" Alma wanted to know, glancing at Helena warily.

"From a baby," Caroline said, "she never story to me."

Lorche fingered her knife in a way that made Helena's scalp prickle. "Missy shall not betray us," Lorche said. "I see to that."

18

Escape

In the black distance, thunder muttered. The horizon flickered with lightning as the forest flickered with flambée-stoks borne by people coming to the Great War Dance. Helena and Caroline watched the people arrive. Their faces, lit by the fires and the torches, reminded Helena of the morning of the revolt. There was something wild in the gleaming eyes, a kind of desperation in the grimacing mouths.

From time to time, Lorche called to them to help. She worked, sweating, over the low-banked cooking fires, grumbling to herself. "Come by here," she would yell at Helena and Caroline. "You lazy gals shall get to work."

Helena and Caroline trotted between the cook fires and the council fires with steaming calabashes of potage or rice or palm-leaf wrapped millet cakes or fire-crisped yams. They pushed their ways through the milling people, and the people grabbed with greedy hands the food they bore. In the red and smoky light, the people looked like specters. Their voices rang dizzyingly in Helena's ears. The fragrance of the spitted pig, the sharp-sweet smell of rum, made Helena's stomach churn. Caroline stuffed handfuls of rice into her mouth and sucked on whelk shells and wild bird bones. But Helena could not eat. Her head whirled, giddy with a single word. Escape! She was going to escape at last.

When the people were hypnotized by Café's dance, Helena and her companions planned to slip away singly to meet on the path above the cliff. A hike of two hours—three at most, Alma assured them— would bring them to the spring in the Company gut. Then they had only to wait for daylight to find their way to Mester Bødker.

"You shall get to work, you shiftless gals," Lorche shouted at them. Shoving loaded platters into their hands, she hissed, "Remember. When Café dances. Remember!"

The people had eaten until their bellies could hold no more. The warriors were bleary and boisterous with rum. The women began to chant. Breffu exhorted them, her dark face savage in the lurid light. And then Helena saw Café stand up and begin to dance.

Helena edged away from the people by the fire. She wandered—nonchalantly, she hoped—toward the group of children who danced a dance of their own around the dying cook fire. The sore-eyed boy was dragging up a rotted branch. By the sparks that leaped up as he flung it on the coals, Helena scanned the children's faces for Lille. She was not there.

"Where is Lille?" Helena asked the sore-eyed boy.

He stared at her blankly and shrugged.

Helena's heart missed a beat.

The boy hopped away, bending and swaying as the warriors did, in a miniature dance of war.

Helena swallowed hard. She tried to think. She was certain Lille had been with the children only a minute before.

As she headed toward Lodama's hut, she saw Alma and Anniche wander in the direction of the privy rocks.

Helena poked her head inside the hut and called in a whisper, "Lille. Lille, where are you?"

There was no answer, no sound at all from the black interior of the hut.

Helena's heart was pounding as she pushed back through the crowd of milling people. Across the camp, she saw Lorche wipe her hands on her ragged shift and turn away from her companions to melt into the shadows of the trees.

Helena searched the face of every child she saw, even babies and great big girls. There were so many people swirling about the campfires—constantly moving, it seemed to Helena—the noise of their voices a gabbling in her ears. The fires threw weird shadows against the trees and huts. Shapes were distorted, colors splashed violent in the shifting light.

There was Caroline! Helena raised her hand to attract Caroline's attention, and Caroline smiled at her, a quavery thin-lipped smile, and waved and disappeared behind a hut. By the time Helena pushed her way through the people to the spot where she had been, Caroline was gone.

A choking lump throbbed in Helena's throat. They had all gone, except her . . . and Lille.

Where was Lille?

Helena forgot to act nonchalant. She ran back to the cook fire and the children dancing there. The sore-eyed boy had overturned a cooking pot. He thumped its battered bottom like a drum.

No Lille!

Helena put her hand to her head and closed her eyes to try to think.

" 'Lena!" came the call, cutting like a knife through the uproar.

Helena opened her eyes and stared in terror. The queen was calling her.

" 'Lena, come by here!"

The imperious voice drew Helena toward the council fire, where Lodama sat with Bolombo and Breffu on stools made of tree trunks, sawed in sections. The people were dancing before them. Through the weaving bodies, Helena caught a glimpse of the royal couple and their retainers. Lodama wore a scarlet bodice and a petticoat of gold and blue.

" 'Lena! 'Lena! Come by here!"

Helena could barely lift her feet to place them one before the other. The queen was calling her. She had to go. She thought of Caroline and Lorche, of Alma and Anniche, waiting on the path above the cliff. How long would they wait, she wondered. The tears in her throat threatened to rise to her eyes. The dancers jostled against her, and she stumbled as she tried to force her way around them to the queen.

Lodama was speaking to her, and now she did not shout, Helena had to bend near to hear.

"This little one should go to bed," Queen Lodama said softly.

Helena gazed open-mouthed at the child in Lodama's lap. Lille curled, thumb in mouth and eyes fast shut, in the folds of the gold and blue petticoat. Helena swallowed hard and lowered her eyes to the ground to keep dizziness from overwhelming her.

"Ya," she said, and it came from her mouth like a croak. She curtsied and grabbed for Lille at one and the same time.

"She sleeps, poor little one," said Lodama, smiling. "The long night and the people and the noise weary her."

"Mange Tak, Queen Lodama," Helena said. She hefted Lille to her shoulder and turned hastily. She staggered as she hurried away from the queen, and thought she could feel Breffu's eyes on her, looking through her skin, searching out her secrets and her thoughts. She clutched the sleeping Lille and pushed her way through the people. Her legs wobbled, threatening to give way.

Now, ahead of her, was Lodama's hut. She chanced a backward glance at the council fire. Breffu was bent to Bolombo, her face intense. Lodama swayed with the singers, eyes half-closed.

Helena began to run—knowing she should not run—past the hut and toward the trees. Behind her the drums beat, and the people shouted in the ruddy glow of the fires. Ahead of her loomed the forest blackness and the welcoming forest hush.

19

The Soldiers

Morning came with the trill of a bird, clear and sweet in the pearly sky. Helena stood up and stretched the stiffness from her limbs, reaching her arms to the first golden rays of the sun coming up over East End ridge. The sun took away the terror of the night, of the stumbling, fumbling hike along the pitch black trail, of the unknown things, wet and wispy that touched her in the dark. The sun brought back the comfortable green of the forest. It turned shadows mossy and leaves emerald. It changed the openings between the trees to sea-water clarity, flecked with motes of gold.

Beside them, the spring splashed singing over its rocks. The bird trilled again, and a chorus of birds took up the song and began the day.

Helena was ravenously hungry. Never, she was sure, had she been so hungry—not even in the camp at van Stell's Point. And she was not at all tired, despite the fact she had scarcely slept. She twirled in an awkward, precarious dance on the flat rocks by the spring.

The others stirred, and Lorche groaned.

"These old bones be glad to get home," she grumbled.

Caroline sat up, rubbing her eyes. She looked a little frightened to realize where she was.

"It far to Coral Bay?" she asked.

"Not far," Alma said. "You certain, Missy, you not let the masters flog us?"

"Oh, yes," Helena said happily. "I won't let them hurt you."

Helena knelt by the spring and splashed water in her face. She unwrapped the rag she had wound about her head to keep her hair from catching in the brush and combed her hair with her fingers. It would be good to wash it with soap, she thought, and have it combed and properly curled. She laughed to herself tc think what Mama would say when she saw it looking so wild.

Helena cupped her hands and took a long, slurping drink from the spring. "Let us go," she urged. "The day advances."

While the other women were drinking and washing at the spring, Helena roused Lille and took her into the brush to urinate. When they came back, she washed the little girl's face and hands. Caroline shared some tamarind pods she had shinnied up a tree to pick. Lille's face had to be washed again when she had eaten hers. But at last they were ready to go.

Alma pointed the way down the gut trail. "Missy go first," she said.

Lille was in high spirits. She seemed to regard the journey as an outing designed specifically for her pleasure. She jabbered to herself and Helena in a language half-babble, half-speech. Trotting ahead of the women as they picked their way down the rocky slope, she discovered treasures—a black and red caterpiller, a crimson leaf, a whorling snail shell—and brought them back for Helena's admiration.

Helena's stomach bubbled with excitement. Everything looked beautiful to her, new-washed and green in the dewy morning. She exclaimed over Lille's discoveries and wondered how she could have imagined the forest was a terrifying place.

But it was not long before she realized the others were not so lighthearted. When she looked back, she saw Alma and Anniche mutter to one another, frowning. Caroline's eyes searched the brush and trail ahead with quick, nervous glances. Lorche had drawn her knife and advanced, almost crouching, down the path.

Helena could still hear the splashing of the spring behind them when the women froze. She felt their sudden stillness, the sharp intake of their breathing, before she herself heard the new noise.

Over the silvery sounds of water and birdsong, over the soft soughing of the breeze, over Lille's squeals and chuckles, Helena heard voices: the deep loud voices of men, wafted up the gut by the wind. And with the voices was a clanking and creaking of metal weapons and leather boots.

For a moment, Helena's own heart turned in fright. Then . . . What am I thinking of, she thought. Those are my people. The soldiers from the bay. Perhaps Mester Bødker is with them. She turned, frowning, to the others. "Come," she said. "It is the soldiers, the soldiers we seek. Don't be afraid."

Alma and Anniche looked at one another. Caroline still seemed frozen, her eyes white and staring, and her mouth trembled a little. Lorche gazed at the knife in her hand intently. She weighed it on her palm and then looked up at Helena.

"Missy *shall* swear Lorche faithful," Lorche said, her voice hard.

"Of course I will," Helena said. "Come. Why do you falter? This is why we ran away—to find the soldiers. Let us go to them."

Lorche put the knife inside her shift, hiding it carefully. "You shall come, you silly gals," she said to the others, and gave Caroline a little shove.

Lille was pulling on the tail of Helena's shirt. Helena stooped and picked her up and started eagerly on. She could hear the voices growing closer. She thought they spoke Danish, but she could not be sure.

The trail opened onto a glade, a narrow, grass-covered shelf at the edge of the forest. Below the glade, the trail wound down a steep slope of low scrub brush and clumps of grass.

The soldiers were just starting up this slope when Helena caught sight of them. Flags fluttered over their heads, red and blue streaming in the wind. Helena recognized the familiar Dannebrog, the Danish sea flag, and the Union Jack of the Britishers. She squinted her eyes to make out the faces of the men. Those in front were white, but black troops climbed behind them. She recognized no one, but then, they were still far away.

Alma and Anniche, Lorche and Caroline crowded behind her. Helena could feel their fright like a chill at her back. She stepped out of the shade of the trees and lifted her arm to wave. She heard the women gasp at her sudden movement and shuffle their feet nervously.

"Hallo!" Helena shouted. She shifted Lille on her hip and stepped forward impulsively, waving her arm. "Hallo. Hallo!" she called.

She saw the soldiers stop and lift their faces to look up the slope.

"Come," she said to the others. "Come with me." She began to walk quickly across the glade, almost running in her eagerness.

The explosion halted her in mid-stride. Before she could understand what was happening, the screaming began behind her. She whirled, glancing wildly at the others.

Anniche and Alma were disappearing into the forest behind the flash of Lorche's gray shift. Caroline had fallen, kicking in the grass, her screams ululating thin and shrill against the clamor of shouts and stamping boots that swept toward them up the trail.

"Nej!" Helena screamed. "Nej, don't fire!"

She saw a musket raised and the curl of smoke that puffed from its muzzle. A bullet furrowed the dirt at her feet. She threw herself away from it, cushioning Lille beneath her as she fell.

"Holde op!" she screamed. "I am Magistrate Sødtmann's daughter!" Her voice was lost in the uproar of the soldiers and of Caroline's screams.

Lille's arms were strangling her. Lille's fingers were digging into her flesh. Lille was wailing in terror. The wailing drowned Helena's thoughts. The ground shook with the thudding of the soldier's running feet.

Helena tried to rise, to stumble toward the bleeding Caroline. Something shrieked past her head, and she fell again. Her ear stung, and she raised her hand to it. She stared in disbelief at the hand, smeared with blood.

Helena looked frantically toward Caroline. Caroline's legs were twitching, but her screams had stopped. At Helena's center, something broke. She turned her face from Caroline and sobbed and struggled to her feet. She ran, clutching Lille in her arms, toward the safety of the forest. Behind her, she heard the crash of musket fire and the curses of the soldiers. Branches whipped her face. Rocks and roots tripped her feet. Brambles grasped her legs and tore at them. Helena ran and ran until the only sounds in her ears were Lille's sobbing and her own and the thudding of her heart.

Daylight was failing when Helena staggered into the women's camp. The light of its fires pricked the grayness of the darkening campground with sparks of warmth. Helena stumbled toward them numbly, too weary to feel relief at having found her way or anxiety over her reception. Her eyes were swollen, her sight dim with crying. Lille shivered and whimpered on her back, never loosening for a moment her strangling grip around Helena's neck. Helena wanted only to sink down beside the warmth of a fire to sleep again as she and Lille had slept, hiding in the brush, through the heat of the day. She fell to her knees and tried to unclasp Lille's clinging arms. Around her, she heard a babble of voices. Someone lifted Lille from her back, and she fell forward and curled herself into a ball within the circle of the fire's warmth.

Hard fingers dug into her shoulder and shook her roughly. She heard Lorche's voice and squeezed her eyes tighter shut against its assault. She felt Lorche's breath on her face and smelled its sour smell.

"Missy," Lorche was saying, "we glad to see you." There was a gasping urgency to Lorche's words. They came in a rush and loudly, spoken directly into Helena's ear. "We tell how we go to carry water this morning, Missy. How we leave before day—Alma and Anniche and Missy and Caroline and me. We tell 'bout soldier mans coming on us at the cistern. You know, Missy, the cistern at Kob plantage."

Slowly, Helena opened her eyes and focused them on Lorche's face, thrust menacingly close to hers. What was Lorche saying?

"When you don't come back all day, we think you go with the soldier mans or they kill you too, like they kill poor Caroline."

Helena finally understood. Lorche had invented a story to conceal the fact they had run away.

Lorche's fingers griped Helena's shoulder. "We *so* glad they not get you, Missy," Lorche said, leering into her face.

"They didn't get me," Helena said. She rolled away from Lorche's sour breath. She buried her face in her arms and shut her eyes.

20

The Sore-Eyed Boy

The thunder and lightning the night of the Great War Dance had not brought rain, any more than the War Dance brought war. Day after day dawned sunny and hot, drying up the gardens and rotting the last fruit fallen from the trees. The women found less and less to harvest on the plantages. The last coconuts were eaten, and even the soursops and the tamarind pods grew scarce. The shoots of millet in Helena's field wilted and browned. The children had to go farther and farther from camp to find lizards and birds for their snares. The people began to be hungry. The streambed in the gut was dusty. The moss on the cliff turned brown.

Helena lay on a pallet in a patch of shade beside the queen's hut day after day. She did not feel sick exactly. In fact, she did not feel anything. The effort of sitting up or walking took more energy than she could find.

One day she heard Lodama tell Breffu to leave Helena alone. " 'Lena sick," Lodama said. "Do not trouble her."

Helena peeked at Breffu's scowling face.

"What make the soldiers leave the missy behind?" Breffu wanted to know. "She their own."

"Study her," Lodama said. "Think you she favor a white child?"

Helena felt Breffu's eyes on her. Embarrassed, she looked down at herself. Her arms and legs, once so softly rounded and white, now were thin and scarred and brown. The remnants of the cambric shirt she wore were torn and filthy. When they met the soldiers near the spring, she remembered, her light hair had been covered by a rag and she had held in her arms a small black child. Who, at that distance, could have seen the blue of her eyes in a face she imagined was as brown as her arms and legs. Why had she not thought of it before? She looked like a slave! Café's skin was no darker than hers. None of the blacks were any dirtier, any more lice-infested, any more ragged than she was.

Breffu had started laughing, an ugly, chuckling laugh. She rose and turned away. "That no white child for true," Breffu said and laughed again.

When Lodama had food brought to Helena, Helena had no will to eat it. Only when Lille sat beside her, coaxing tidbits into her mouth, did Helena make the attempt to chew and swallow.

At night, Lille crawled onto the pallet next to her and snuggled against her, warm and soft. Helena was as apt to lie awake, staring into the darkness of the hut at night as she was to sleep through most of the day, oblivious to the comings and goings around her.

At first, Helena had not been able to think. Later she willed it so. She did not hurt, but neither could she find comfort. Only Lille could make her smile.

Then, one day, Lodama brought news. She sat beside Helena and stroked her face. She looked into Helena's eyes. "You must hear me, 'Lena," Queen Lodama said. "You must know what I say. We got word of Caroline. The soldiers carry her to Mester Bødker at the vaern. He take a bullet from her back and tend her. She at the vaern. Alive. Do you hear it, 'Lena? Caroline alive."

Helena watched Lodama's lips carefully as she spoke. The words arranged and rearranged themselves in Helena's mind. Helena could catch hold of one or two, but when she tried to make sense of them, they slipped away. She blinked and looked into Lodama's brown eyes, fixed sympathetically on her face.

"Caroline alive," Lodama repeated, slowly and softly.

Helena stared at her, her face working as gradually the meaning came to her. Then tears rolled down her cheeks and sobs tore at her throat. The tears washed away the fog in her head and let in the pain, clear and bright. She cried and cried, and Lodama rocked her in her arms.

. . .

The sore-eyed boy could no longer see at all. Helena found the other children tormenting him one day, pelting him with sticks and clods of earth. They taunted him in a cruel sort of blind man's bluff.

"Shame! Shame on you." Helena chased away the squealing children and took the sobbing little boy into her lap. She cleaned his oozing eyes as best she could with a not-too-dirty rag.

"Hush, hush," she crooned to him, rocking him in her arms as Lodama had rocked her.

Lille squatted beside them and patted him with her tiny, pink-palmed hand. She made crooning sounds, imitating Helena.

"I will take care of the sore-eyed little boy also," Helena told the queen.

"You need a hut of your own, 'Lena, if you got more children," Lodama said.

The hut of her own was not so large as the queen's, but no one slept in it except Helena and Lille and the little boy. Helena cleaned it out with a broom made of twigs. She fashioned fresh pallets of rustling plantain leaves, a larger one for herself and two small ones for the children. But Lille still crawled onto Helena's pallet in the dark of night, and Helena did not send her away. She liked to wake in the night to the warmth of Lille against her and the sound of her breathing. Now also there was the labored wheeze of the little boy nearby.

There was no water for washing, but Helena kept the children as neat as she could. Lodama showed her how to plait Lille's wooly hair in rows, and she kept the lice picked from their scalps. Several times a day, she cleaned the little boy's mattering eyes.

The sore-eyed boy was always hurting himself. He collided with people and trees and huts. He tripped over baskets and pots on the ground. Helena was afraid he would fall into a fire. She remembered the leading strings of her old childish frocks and made something like them from long strips of rag tied like a harness around his scrawny shoulders. Soon, everywhere Helena went, the little boy followed, attached by his leading strings. And Lille trotted beside her, or rode on her back.

A few days after Helena learned Caroline was alive, the death wails sounded in the women's camp. Kanta's warriors had fought a "batterie," as the bussals called it, with a force of free negroes. They had run out of powder and retreated, carrying wounded and dead. The people did not gather at the fires that night to sing and dance. Helena fell asleep listening to the mourning women chant their grief.

Helena seldom thought now about any other life. Her days were filled with caring for her children and scrounging food for them. There was a pain around her heart when she thought of Caroline.

"It was my fault, you see," she said to Lille and the little boy when the pain made it necessary to tell someone what she felt. "It was my fault Caroline got hurt," she said, and they listened, though she knew they did not understand. "I told her I would protect her, and I didn't," Helena said. "I couldn't. They shot at me. At me!"

Lille stuck her thumb in her mouth and looked sad. Perhaps, Helena thought, she could tell from Helena's voice that something was not right. Lille's eyes did not leave Helena's face.

"At least Queen Lodama is kind, even though my own people shoot at me," Helena said. "And you love me, don't you, my little ones?"

Lille crawled into her lap, and the little boy scrunched closer. She put her arm around him.

"Of course, the soliders didn't know who I was," she said. "But they shouldn't have fired nonetheless. We were only girls and women. There was no harm in us. It is not right to hurt helpless people," Helena said sternly. "I am certain my mama would be very angry if she knew . . ." Helena sighed. She wondered how angry Mama would truly be to know a ragtag group of slave women had been fired upon. "I am certain," Helena said, "my mama misses me very much." She thought—and pushed away the thought before it formed itself into words—that Mama would scarcely know what to make of her now, now she saw things by such a different light.

Pain pressed hard around Helena's heart. "She *did* go away and leave me," Helena said, and her voice was almost a whisper.

The warriors began to return to the women's camp. Helena heard rumors that the leaders had decided it was time for battle. At night, Breffu and Café whipped the men to a frenzy with rum and dancing. Bolombo made speeches, urging the warriors to ready their weapons. Prince Aquashi boasted and strutted before his men. Kanta, licking his wounds, moved back to the women's camp.

A sudden storm blew up. The rain turned the dusty campground to mud. The women set out pots and calabashes to catch the water and lifted their mouths to the sky to drink. Helena took her children out into the downpour and stripped and scrubbed them as best she could with maran leaves until their skins were raw and pink and they whimpered and struggled to escape her ministrations.

After two days, the rain ended as abruptly as it had begun. By midmorning, the mud was drying in all but the shadiest places. The sun sucked the moisture from the roofs of the steaming huts. The stream in the gut diminished to a trickle. The tender green of newly sprouted plants yellowed and drooped beneath the onslaught of the sun.

Helena watched as the warrior, Cotompa, and a handful of men left the camp. Breffu and Bolombo strode about issuing orders and marshalling the other men.

By afternoon, Cotompa was back, flourishing two grisly, fair-haired heads on poles. Helena, mending the roof of her hut where the rain had washed away the mud plaster, heard the commotion and left her work. She glimpsed the heads and turned away quickly, her stomach rising to her throat. Then she went back to mending her hut and tried not to hear the jubilant shouting that told of another batterie, a batterie won this time with the killing of three whites and the fleeing of their fellows.

Helena heard the victory celebration deep into the night, long after she had finished her work and found food for the children and put them to bed. She lay on her pallet in the dark and listened to the unearthly sounds of the warriors' jubilee, and her stomach felt sick, and her mouth tasted bitter.

In the following days, Helena tried to be invisible. She took the children into the forest to search for food. When they found only a few overripe soursops, Helena pilfered some watery gruel from the cook women. In the evenings, she kept the children in her hut, inventing stories to keep them amused. The stories served another purpose. They kept her from thinking or feeling too much.

21

The Lizard

The sore-eyed boy had made a lizard trap.

"I can do it," he had insisted. "I make traps before time."

"But before, you could see," Helena said.

"Don't need no eyes, only hands," the little boy said, and it was true. The trap formed itself beneath his quick and clever fingers, not much more lumpy and ragged-looking than the traps the other children made.

The lizard trap was a sort of long, narrow funnel, woven of pliable strips of cane. When a lizard, or other small animal, ventured into its open, wider end in search of shade, or perhaps from curiosity, the pliable sides would draw tight about its body, and it would be unable to turn around to escape.

"I catch us lizards to eat," the sore-eyed boy boasted.

Helena did not contradict him, but she did not think it likely. She had not seen a lizard near the camp for a long, long time. All the lizards have been eaten by now, she thought. Sometimes she wished them back, not to eat, but so *they* would eat the mosquitoes that swarmed after rain.

Now, however, there was no rain either. Although Helena figured it must be nearing Easter, rain was another thing they had not seen for a long, long time. Helena tried to count the days and weeks she had lived in the women's camp. She soon gave up. Time had blurred into a pattern of sameness, distinguishable only as "when-Caroline-was-here" and "after-they-caught-Caroline."

The days burned winter-hot and windy, like the blast of a boiling house furnace. In the forest, the fallen leaves of drought-stricken trees made a rustling carpet on the ground. The evergreen cinnamon bays curled their dry leaves to endure the sun. The air plants and orchids clung shriveled to bare branches of genip and dog-almond trees. In open places, the grass was burned brown and crisp.

The children were always hungry.

Now that the men were firmly established in the women's camp, Breffu's strictly impartial distribution of food had been abandoned. Whatever little food the women found each day was eaten by the men. The women learned to hoard a portion of their gleanings for themselves to supplement the scanty leftovers they were allowed. But Helena was not very successful at finding things to eat. Without Caroline's help, she did not know where to dig for edible roots or how to capture small animals and birds. She could not bring herself to tear apart the huge mud termites' nests or dig into anthills for insects to eat. And the fruits and berries and garden crops she had used to gather were no longer to be found in the parched forest and fields.

One day, Helena left Lille and the little boy in the care of an old woman. Word had come that the Turk's head cacti were beginning to fruit. Aba was going to lead a group of women to the place where they grew.

"It far," she told Helena, "and you weak from hunger. More better leave your children in camp."

All day, as she grappled with the prickly cacti in the hot, dry wind, Helena felt anxious about the children. She had not been separated from Lille since she took charge of her on the trek from van Stell's Point. She was glad when Aba said it was time to turn homeward. Going back, she thought the women moved slowly and stupidly. But she had to admit she could have gone no faster by herself.

The slingful of cactus fruit on her back pulled achingly against the tumpline on her forehead. She wished she knew how to carry baskets on her head like Aba and some of the other bussals. They could walk gracefully upright, instead of straining forward as she did, to balance the load on her back.

They dragged into the women's camp in the hottest hour of the afternoon. An old man opened one eye as they trooped past his resting place and brushed away a fly before he fell asleep again. From a far hut, a baby whined. The air droned with insects and the snores of the men. It smelled of dust.

Helena looked for the children, but did not see them.

Near the cookfire, the women unloaded their day's harvest of immature cactus fruit. Aba helped Helena slip out of her sling by lifting it off her back. The cook-women began to sort and count the fruit. Helena turned away to find Lille and the little boy. The small bag of fruit she had hidden beneath her shirt banged against her hip as she walked. Already some of the fruit gatherers were sprawled in the shade asleep. Helena thought she too would take a nap, as soon as she made certain the children were safe.

She went to the old woman's hut.

"Where are Lille and the sore-eyed boy?" she asked.

The woman shook her head, her eyes cloudy with sleep.

"Didn't you tie the boy out of harm's way as I told you?" Helena demanded. "He cannot be allowed to roam."

The skin of the old woman's throat waggled, loose and wrinkled, beneath her chin.

Helena was suddenly uneasy. She hurried away to her own hut.

"Lille. Boy. I am home. Come see what I have for you," she called.

The children were not playing outside the hut. Perhaps they had crawled inside to sleep. Helena was bending to peer through the doorway when she heard Lille giggle. Relieved, she pulled the bag of fruit from under her shirt, and tucked it inside the hut.

"Lille," Helena called.

Lille came dancing from a nearby thicket, her eyes sparkling. She threw her arms around Helena's knees and then danced away again, tugging at Helena's hand.

" 'Lena shall come by here," she said. "Come. Come."

"Where is our boy?" Helena asked.

"Come, come," Lille said, and Helena let her lead her into the thicket.

Helena had to bend over and duck her head to traverse the path through the brush. Twigs caught in her hair, and a thorn scratched her cheek.

"Come, come," Lille said.

In a moment, Helena had pushed her way into an open place in the undergrowth. Above their heads, the lignum vitae trees arched, branches swaying in the hot wind. The dry leaves rustled like excited whispers.

In the center of the clearing, the sore-eyed boy sat cross-legged on a large, flat stone. He held his back as straight and proud as King Bolombo's. His mattering eyes stared sightlessly over Helena's shoulder, but there was a happy grin on his dusty face. He held his hands before him, offering for Helena's inspection the raggedy woven lizard trap.

"I catch us a lizard to eat," the sore-eyed boy said.

Lille giggled and clapped her hands.

Helena knelt before the rock and took the trap from his hands. From the open end, a slender green tail flicked.

"Why, so you have, you clever boy," Helena said. "You have caught a lizard in your trap."

The boy nodded regally. "I say I catch us a lizard," he said.

Helena knew the tiny lizard would make only a bite or two for each of them, but it would taste good. And the sightless boy had caught it with a trap he made himself. She reached to give him a squeeze, and he slid from the rock to sit beside her, his hand on her arm. Lille squatted on her haunches, surveying them gleefully.

"*You* shall kill my lizard," the little boy said, as though conferring a great favor. He laid down a jagged stone.

"Very well," Helena said.

She reached into the narrow opening of the woven funnel with the fingers of one hand and grasped the fragile body of the lizard. It wriggled in her hand as she expanded the mouth of the trap and pulled it out.

The pale green skin of the lizard was so thin, she could almost see the delicate bones beneath it. The long tail lashed. The tiny knobbed toes splayed out like fingers. Helena could feel the lizard's heart pulse against her palm.

She knew she did not even need the rock. All she had to do was squeeze the lizard in her hand to crush out its life.

The lizard cocked its head and fixed her with an eye as hard and shiny as Mama's jet earbobs. It flared its throat in crimson challenge and flickered its tongue defiantly.

Helena's heart turned. The lizard felt so vulnerable in her hand . . . and looked so brave . . .

"Kill it," said the little boy.

"Kill, kill," babbled Lille, bouncing on her heels.

The lizard regarded Helena with what seemed to her to be desperation. The scarlet throat swelled and trembled. The tiny heart throbbed.

Helena's fingers loosened imperceptibly.

For an instant, the lizard poised on her hand. Then, with a flick of its tail, it was gone.

"Oh!" wailed Lille. "Oh, oh!"

"What happens?" cried the sore-eyed boy, clutching Helena's arm.

"It escaped me," Helena said. "I am sorry. It escaped."

The sore-eyed boy began to cry. Helena pulled him and Lille close.

"Hush, hush," she said. "I have some cactus fruit to eat. You will catch another lizard in your trap. It is a splendid, wonderful trap. Do not cry."

Helena's eyes searched the ground and nearby brush for the flash of a pale green lizard's tail while she held the children close and tried to comfort them. And all the time, she was wishing she could see the lizard once again . . . Running free.

22

The Last Batterie

Breffu was being prepared for battle.

She stood in the sunlight before the queen's hut while Lodama and the Adampe noblewomen, Alette and Sara and Suplica, bathed her from a calabash of precious water. The noblewomen washed her and dried her and oiled her skin with palm oil until it gleamed like black satin. They wrapped a loincloth of spotless white about her hips and draped her body from waist to foot in an undergarment of thin linen.

Helena, watching, wondered where they had gotten the clean, whole cloth. Had it been saved for just this day?

Lodama brought forth a loose, open robe of canary silk, which she hung about Breffu's shoulders.

Helena could not imagine how Breffu planned to fight, swathed in so many folds of clothing. Perhaps the king did not really expect her to do battle. Perhaps she was being allowed to take part as a kind of talisman for the army. Yet Breffu was so ferocious-appearing, Helena could not imagine her being kept from fighting. She decided the garments must serve a ceremonial purpose, like Papa Sødtmann's dress sword, and would be shed when the fighting began.

Now Breffu knelt on a mat, while Lodama dressed her hair. The queen plaited the oiled black tresses in intricate patterns, ornamented with shells and beads and shining bits of metal. And she tied a battle charm about Breffu's neck.

Café was mixing colored pigments in coconut shells. Using her slender fingertips, she painted Breffu's face, red and blue and white, highlighting the scarified insignia of Breffu's rank and tribe.

Breffu's face was impassive. Her eyes had a trancelike, unfocused look. She did not speak.

At last, the noblewomen stepped away.

Breffu stood to her full height, her arms outstretched from her sides. The canary robe shimmered and swayed. The ornaments in her hair caught the light.

The women murmured, and even Helena caught her breath. The proud set of Breffu's broad shoulders, the noble lines of her square jaw and muscular neck struck Helena as beautiful. Helena hated Breffu and feared her, but now she had to admire her, too. The warrior woman shone with a fierce, steady power— with strength and dignity.

King Bolombo advanced across the campground

with measured steps. His tattooed face was painted like Breffu's. His robe was black and red. He carried a musket, which he placed in Breffu's hands. Again the women murmured.

Bolombo led Breffu to where the warriors waited. Each man was painted and bedecked with feathers and shells. The higher-ranking fighters shouldered muskets. The others carried sugar cane knives and captured swords.

Prince Aquashi and Kanta stepped from the ranks to join Breffu and the king.

The women and children were quiet, dazzled by the warrior army. Helena found herself holding her breath. The sore-eyed boy did not ask what was happening. He seemed to sense the awesomeness of the moment.

Bolombo raised his hand, and his voice rang out.

"I Bolombo, your king," he said, "*I* shall lead you in this batterie."

"Bolombo, Bolombo!" the warriors shouted.

"Aquashi, your mighty prince. *He* shall lead you in this batterie."

"Aquashi, Aquashi!" the warriors shouted.

"Kanta, the conqueror of the white mans' fort. *He* shall lead you in this batterie."

"Kanta, Kanta!" the warriors shouted.

"Lady Breffu, a true warrior-woman. With her own hand did she kill the masters. *Breffu* shall lead you in this batterie!"

For a moment there was silence.

Then, "Breffu, Breffu, Breffu!" shouted the warriors.

The voices of the women joined them, and the shout became a roar. "Bolombo! Aquashi! Kanta! Breffu!"

Above the roar rose the powerful voice of the king. "This time, the masters shall die!" he cried. "This time, the people shall go free!"

He turned on his heel and marched away, up the mountain trail. Aquashi and Kanta and Breffu went behind him, and behind them, the warriors marched and chanted, "Free! Free! Free!"

The old women mumbled charms. Someone killed a black chicken—obtained from who knew where—and staked it to the ground in the center of the camp, its belly slit open, its entrails spilling in the dust. The flies buzzed over the bloody carcass. The ants made trails to it in the dirt.

At dawn the next day, the women's camp was awake and listening. The women did not go out to gather food.

"We need food for the victory feast," Helena heard the queen say.

But the women did not go out. They waited and listened, silent and tense. Helena saw fear in their eyes.

The hours of the morning crept by. The heat built in waves. The wind blew unnervingly in the trees.

Lodama, her belly big now with child, sat in the doorway of her hut, where everyone could see her. Her face was unworried. She scraped a calabash clean and dry.

But Helena knew Lodama's tranquillity was feigned, to keep people calm. Helena herself did not know how to feel.

The warriors had been so strong and beautiful, she found herself hoping for their victory. But they were fighting against Helena's own people, she reminded herself—perhaps against Mester Bødker and their neighbors, Herre Suhm and Monsieur Castan and Judge Hendrichsen—certainly against the soldiers sent by Bedstefader.

What would happen if the rebels won? Would the white men go away forever as Bolombo said? Would she never see Mama and Thomas again?

What would happen if the rebels lost? To this Helena knew the answer with sickening certainty. They would never be allowed to go back to the plantages to take up their old slave lives again. They would be tortured and killed for their crimes. Helena remembered the punishment for a runaway slave: the amputation of a leg. She did not like to imagine the punishments for rebel slaves.

She looked at Lille, who was trying to help the sore-eyed boy mend his lizard trap. She looked at the boy, his blind face wrinkled with concentration. She looked at Lodama's smooth, kind face.

"Would you like me to tell you a story?" she whispered to the children, a little desperately. "Let me tell you a story about the little house where we shall live one day, and our pretty red frocks and our silver spoons and our necklaces of shiny blue beads."

The warriors began to drift back into the women's camp in the afternoon. They came in small groups, many bloody and limping from their wounds. Eight of them were carried in, already stiffening with the rigor of death.

The rebel army had fought well, they said, but the white men had many faithful slaves to fight with *them*, and *their* weapons did not misfire, and *their* ammunition did not run out. In the shadowy dawn, the rebels had done much damage. They had burned buildings and fields. They had killed many enemies. But daylight made them easy targets for the barricaded white men, and daylight showed them the white men's strength.

"It the fault of that woman," the warriors said. "She say they fall beneath our knives like cane at harvest time. But they not fall. There too few of us. Our weapons bad. Our hearts feel shame a woman leads us. It the fault of Breffu."

Helena heard their excuses with a strange mixture of satisfaction and outrage. She could not help feeling glad to see Breffu brought low; but she knew in her heart Breffu was unjustly blamed. She is mean and scary, Helena thought, and she is harsh, but I'll wager *she* did not run away. Helena watched and wondered, feeling shaky and bewildered, as the warriors limped in. What would happen now?

Now Lodama did not try to hide her emotions. With the appearance of the first of the dead, she led the mourning relatives in the chants of death, her grieving face streaked with ashes and tears.

The death wails frightened Lille, as they always did. She sucked her thumb and hid her face against Helena's shoulder and whimpered plaintively. The sore-eyed boy asked questions until, distracted, Helena told him sharply to be still. After that, he did not say a word, but sat as far from her as his leading strings would stretch, his hurt and puzzled face reproaching her.

Aquashi and Kanta returned to camp, their faces dark with anger. They gathered up their followers, and by the dawn of the next day, they had deserted the women's camp.

Bolombo and Breffu did not come back. Café and the Adampe noblewomen and most of the Adampe warriors slipped away to join them, Bolombo's witch men among them. The severely wounded were left in the women's camp, with only their women to tend them.

In the confusion of comings and goings, some people simply disappeared. Lorche and Alma and Anniche were seen no more, and no one knew where they had gone.

Queen Lodama, nearing the time for her baby to be born, stayed in the women's camp. Asari stayed with her, his face old now and his shoulders bent. Defeat walked with them and with the few who remained. Helena saw how it stooped their bodies and lined their faces with grief.

Helena did not know what to do. What would become of them? What would become of her?

When Asari told her to, she moved back into Lodama's hut, taking Lille and the little boy with her.

23

Rain

The rain began in the night. Helena woke to its sound on the roof of the hut. She lay awake a long time, listening to the steady downpour. There was no wind, as there had been in the storm at van Stell's Point, only the constant pouring of a heavy spring rain. What we have been needing, Helena had to remind herself as she shifted her pallet to avoid the water leaking through the roof.

She pulled the thin linen covering closer about her shoulders and made sure Lille and the little boy were snug beneath it. She tried not to think about the emptiness of her belly. It would be very unpleasant searching for food tomorrow, if the rain continued. But the rain would make more food grow. The trees would blossom now and set fruit. The fields could be planted. The guts would run with water. She could bathe the children again.

The rain did not let up next day. The campground became a mire. The cookfire smoldered and drowned, hissing in the wet. Helena did wash the children, and then could not get them dry. They huddled, shivering, in their corner of Lodama's hut and watched the gray sheet of rain through the doorway. The water seeped under the walls of the hut and through the thatching of the roof. The packed dirt floor was wet. The pallets felt damp, and so did their scanty rags.

Helena was too miserable to go out to search for food. Lille and the little boy whimpered with hunger, and the queen shared a bit of soggy millet cake with them, then told them stories about Anansesem, the wily spider god.

"Anansesem's third son called River Drinker," she told them with a twinkle in her eye. "If the stream in the gut rise too high, we ask him to take a big drink!"

"No more stream!" Lille giggled.

In the afternoon, Asari came to talk to the queen. Helena was trying to nap with the children, but Asari's low, worried voice brought her fully awake.

From the ridge overlooking Coral Bay, Asari said, he had seen two ships sail into the harbor the afternoon before. "They fly the flag of France," he said. "I myself counted more than two hundred men, most of them white. They have set up tents on the beach and have brought food with them from the ships. They have many guns . . ."

Helena peeked at Asari through the murky light of the hut. He was hunched over, his face in shadow.

"What business do Frenchmen have on a Danish island held by rebellious slaves?" he said. "I do not understand this thing."

"The Frenchmans cruel masters, people say," said Queen Lodama.

"Ya. So it is said."

"Think you they come to help the Danes?"

"I do think it."

Lodama's voice was gentle. She took Asari's hand in hers and looked into his eyes. "What other things think you, my friend?"

Asari lifted his head and returned her look unflinchingly. His voice was also gentle, and so soft, Helena could barely make out the words. "I think it is the end, my queen."

The rain did not break until the next morning. Then, for a few hours, the sun steamed the forest. Asari instructed Helena to stay near camp in her search for food. But near camp, Helena could find little to eat. She did see hesitant first shoots of grass that seemed to grow almost before her eyes. The bay leaves had uncurled to drink the rain. A gurgling stream tumbled in the gut.

For two days, the sun played hide and seek with the rain.

Asari posted a lookout on the ridge above Coral Bay to monitor the movements of the French. They had great quantities of food, the lookout said, but it was too well-guarded to steal. Helena and the others listened hungrily as he told of it.

Shortly after dawn of the third day, the lookout ran into camp, breathless, his eyes staring.

Asari came running from his hut.

"They march, Master Asari," the lookout gasped. "They move out before day, and I not see them go."

"Where are they now?" Asari demanded.

"They take two roads, Master, but both lead to Bourdeaux Mountain."

The women at the cook fire dropped their pots and spoons. A mother ran to find her child.

Asari called to the men. "Warriors, the white man comes," he said. "Who will come with me to Bourdeaux to head them off, so our women have time to escape?"

Shakily, a dozen men stepped forward. Some were old. Two limped with wounds. All were gaunt with hunger, their cheeks sunken, the bones of their ribcages painfully apparent beneath their grayed skins. Their eyes burned feverishly.

Helena saw Asari look at the men. The sorrow in his eyes caught at her heart.

"Come," he said, reaching for his musket, which was rusted, made useless by the rain.

"I will meet you at the place we agreed," Asari said to Lodama. He led the warriors from the camp.

Helena watched the last man disappear up the trail—an old man, who tottered as he tried to run.

Lodama went into the hut and emerged, carrying a bundle. Lille was crying. Helena bent to tie the sore-eyed boy's leading strings to her waist. The other women milled uncertainly. Helena realized how few of them there were.

"You shall go, my children," Lodama said. "Go quickly in all directions except to Bourdeaux plantage. You shall travel two or three together, and carry little with you. You shall find places to hide in the brush and stay quiet until dark."

"But where go we then?" wailed a young woman. "Where?"

Lodama bowed her head. "I know not, child. Only go! Your queen's heart goes with you."

Helena's head ached so it was difficult to focus her eyes. The world kept swimming into a blur. What about me, she thought. What about me?

"You, 'Lena," Lodama said, as if answering the unspoken question. "If you wish it, I take your children, and you wait here for the white mans. I think they come soon. If you shall uncover your hair and wash in the stream white as you can. I think they not harm you."

Wait for the white man. Helena considered the words. No, they would not harm her, she thought, if she was alone and they saw who she was. She tried to envision rescue at last. She tried to imagine a reunion with Mama, as she had imagined it so many times in the last five months. But she could not remember Mama's face. Mama had golden hair and eyes of blue, she told herself. Mama's cheeks were rosy, and her chin was round and dimpled. There was no answering vision. The only eyes Helena saw were eyes of brown.

The only hair was black and curling. The only cheeks and chin were embossed with delicate, raised tatoos. Lodama's face. Lodama, standing alone—needing me, Helena thought.

"I will go with you, Queen Lodama," Helena said.

They saw the smoke of the burning women's camp from the high ground of the deserted plantage where they stopped for water. They had headed into the brush, taking turns to hack a path with a heavy cane knife, but had soon come upon the overgrown trail that led them to the roofless ruins of the plantage.

The smoke rose into the air and joined black clouds, sweeping in from the sea. Helena wondered about Asari and the warriors. They had not stopped the Frenchmen for long, it seemed.

Lodama held her hand against her swollen belly. She breathed in gasps as she watched the smoke. Helena saw her close her eyes.

"Let us go," she said when she opened them again.

It began to rain as they walked away from the ruined plantage, heading southwest into the forest.

24

The Pools

Asari was waiting for them. Helena saw how Lodama sagged against him as he half-carried her through the brush, along an almost invisible pathway. A moment later, he was back again. He lifted Lille from Helena's back and took the staggering sore-eyed boy's hand. Helena followed them, the dripping branches beside the path soaking her again and again as she pushed between them. The rain ran steadily into her eyes, and her sodden hair weighed on her neck.

The path opened into a tiny clearing, which contained a hut. Asari pushed the children and Helena before him through the doorway of the hut, then stooped and crawled in after them.

In the dim interior, Helena could see Lodama lying, eyes shut, her chest rising and falling heavily, on a pallet against the far wall. Asari crawled to her and began to rub her arms and legs with cloths. Helena knelt, catching her breath, and reveled in the dryness of the hut. Outside, the rain whispered, and water flowed, splashing nearby; but inside the hut, Helena could wipe the rain from her eyes and breathe the close, musty air.

The sore-eyed boy coughed, a barking cough acquired in the last several hours. Helena reached for one of Asari's cloths and began to wipe the children with it. Beneath her fingers, the little boy's skin felt hot. His eyelids were sealed shut with matter. Helena tried to clean his eyes, but he whimpered and twisted away from her. She stripped off Lille's rags and rubbed her with the cloth until her skin glowed, then scrubbed the wetness from her plaited hair and wrapped her in another dry rag.

"I feared for you," Asari said.

"We traveled slowly," Helena said, when Lodama did not answer him. "The queen is not well, as you can see. She had to rest often. And the children could not go fast. I think my little boy is sick."

Asari put his thin, strong hand on the forehead of the little boy. The child moaned and tossed his head fretfully. He coughed, his distended abdomen and spindly arms and legs wracked with the spasms.

Asari looked grave. He shook his head.

When the children had been dried, Helena took off her own dripping shirt and wrung out her hair. A delicious smell came from a vessel heating on a clay pot filled with hot coals.

"Food?" she whispered, scarcely believing it, and Asari scooped rice gruel onto a banana leaf and handed it to her.

"I stored supplies here a long time ago," he said, "when I built this shelter. There is not much, but enough for a few days."

While Helena and Lille stuffed the gruel into their mouths greedily, Helena looked about her at the tight, neatly constructed walls and thickly thatched ceiling of the hut. It was as good a hut as a woman could build, she thought. Had Asari known they would come here someday? She watched Asari help Lodama to sit up and eat some gruel. She remembered when he had nursed her long ago. He was as good as a woman in many womanly things.

After a few mouthfuls, Helena's shrunken stomach could take no more. She tried to force a few grains of rice between the little boy's lips, but he would not swallow them. Instead, he curled himself into a ball on the floor of the hut.

"Sleep," he moaned. "Sleep."

Helena wanted to ask Asari if he and the warriors from the camp had met the Frenchmen from the ships. But she could not seem to keep her eyes open. Comfort spread sleepiness from the fullness of her stomach to her warm, dry toes and fingertips. Her tongue was thick with sleep as she tried to ask, and she felt herself sliding down to the pallet. I will sleep now and talk later, she thought. Asari will keep watch. She felt Lille snuggle into the curve of her body. She felt the restless tossing of the little boy. When he rolled against Helena, she felt the fever of his skin, even in her sleep.

Helena roused once to the murmur of Asari's voice and Lodama's. They spoke a language she did not know.

Another time, she opened her eyes to the scream of a night-flying bird. The hut was dark. Lille's leg was thrown across hers, heavy for a thing so small. The labored breathing of the little boy, and his choking cough, came from nearby. She slept uneasily after that, her dreams awhirl with color and heat and noise....

She thought she should get up to tend the little boy, but her body was pressed to the pallet by leaden weights. She could not open her eyes. She dreamed of the sun, scorching her skin to blisters that broke and drained wetness over her. She dreamed of blood and of rain filling her nose and mouth so she could not breathe. And then her mouth was filled with food—rich chicken stew, meaty and hot, and the sweetness of a mango whose juice ran down her chin, sticky and cool. And then she was trying to give some of the mango to the starving baby, but the baby only cried and turned away his head, and made a strange, gurgling sound in his throat....

When she woke, sunlight streamed outside the doorway, gilding the mist that rose from the sodden ground.

Helena was alone in the hut, except for the sleeping Lille. Carefully, Helena sat up and moved away from the little girl so as not to wake her.

She reached into the vessel of gruel, now cold, and scraped a few dried grains from the bottom of the pot. Then she crawled outside.

The sun shone through an opening in the thick, gray clouds that roiled in the morning sky. A silver sheet of rain fell from the clouds onto another part of the island, but here the sun warmed her skin. She unwound the rag from her damp hair and fluffed it in the sunlight to dry. Then she followed the path through the brush toward the voices she heard over splashing water nearby.

The rain had mired the steep path treacherously. Helena had to feel for firm footing and hold onto the soaking branches and the slippery trunks of trees as she moved.

Then, suddenly, the sun was reflecting brilliance into her eyes. A waterfall splashed from the cliff above into a wide, shallow pool at her feet. That pool was fed by a tumbling stream from two other pools above, cradled in hollows of the sloping sandstone hillside. Slender gray trees, misted with new green, overhung the pools. They swayed in the morning breeze and shook down showers of silver droplets onto the limpid brown surface of the water.

Helena caught her breath with the beauty of it.

Then she saw Asari and Lodama kneeling on a flat stone shelf beside the middle pool. The sore-eyed little boy lay between them on the sun-dried rock. He looked strangely quiet to Helena, his knees pulled up stiffly to his chest.

"Hallo," Helena said. "Is my little boy better?"

She scrambled up toward them over the rocks, slipping on a shaded, still-wet stone. When she regained her balance and looked at Lodama and Asari again, their eyes were turned to her.

They are sad, Helena thought. Perhaps he is no better. Perhaps...

Lodama held out her arms.

"What do you do to him?" Helena cried, suddenly afraid.

"We wash him, child," Lodama said.

"To bring down his fever?" Helena said, hopefully.

"He has no more fever," said Asari.

Helena had reached them. She ignored Lodama's outstretched arms and put her hand on the little boy's head.

"Good," she said. "Perhaps he's getting well—"

Her throat closed on the last word; she snatched back her hand and stared hard at the sore-eyed little boy. There was an utter stillness to his face. The lips were slightly parted, the eyes sealed shut. Drops of water sparkled on his skin where Lodama had been washing him. His arms and legs looked like broken sticks. His head seemed much too large.

"He gone, child," Lodama said.

Gone. Helena reached out again and touched his face. The skin felt cold to her fingers, cold and firm—too firm. There was no movement in his face— no life.

"You mean dead," Helena said, her voice flat among the trills of singing birds. She did not take her eyes from the little boy's face, but she drew her hand away.

"I found him thus this morning," Asari said. "He died while we slept."

"I thought you were watching," Helena accused.

"I slept," said Asari.

Lodama touched Helena gently. She stroked her arm, but Helena shook her hand off.

"He gone to his homeland, child, to Africa. When we die, us Africans, we born again soon in Africa. In Africa, he see again. In Africa, he free."

"He never lived in Africa," Helena said bitterly. "He was born right here on St. Jan. He wouldn't know what to do in Africa. He wouldn't have anyone there to take care of him."

"He find a mother to take care of him in Africa. He did find you, 'Lena, and you did take good care."

A tear burned in Helena's eye. She blinked to keep it back, but it spilled onto her cheek and scalded a pathway to the corner of her mouth. She tasted its salt on her tongue.

Lodama was sloshing the clear, warm water from the pool over the emaciated little body on the rock.

"We wash him now and give him burial," she said.

Helena cleared her throat.

"Let me bathe his eyes," she said. "I know how to do it so it doesn't hurt."

It began to rain again as Asari placed the little body in the shallow grave. Water seeped into the bottom of the grave, and Helena shuddered to think how cold and wet the grave would be.

The little boy was wrapped in a linen cloth, curled on his side as though asleep. He looked so . . . small.

"Wait," Helena said.

She ran back to the pools, to the clump of spider lilies she remembered blooming on the rocky slope. She broke off a white, spiky blossom and took it back to the grave, where she knelt and laid it beside the little boy.

"There," she said. "I wish he had his lizard trap. He was so proud of it."

The rain rattled on the leaves of the trees and plopped steadily in great squelching drops into the mud. Helena did not help to cover the body with palm fronds and wet dirt. She did not help pile stones in a mound over the grave. She watched as Asari and Lodama did these things, and the raindrops coursed over her face like tears.

25

Waiting

Asari was carving something into the smooth stone above the upper pool. It was a little like writing and more like pictures than writing—yet truly neither. Whenever the rain cleared, Asari took his knife and his hard, sharpened sticks of gregre wood and worked at his carvings. He crouched over them hours at a time, stopping only when the rain poured into his eyes and made the surface of the stone too slick to carve.

"What is it?" Helena asked. "What does it mean?"

"It is the story of this time," Asari said.

"It doesn't *look* like a story," said Helena. "*I* can't read it."

"It is not for whites," Asari said shortly, and Helena felt affronted.

She did not ask him about the carvings again,

but she watched him sometimes from the corners of her eyes, when she sat with Queen Lodama on the rocks.

The queen grew more tranced, more dreaming, every day. She slept and slept and woke to eat and slept again. When she was awake, she sat, rocking her body to and fro gently, her eyes fixed on a distance Helena could not see. What Helena could see were the movements of the child within Lodama—small ripplings of the skin of her belly, or larger, more emphatic undulations of her flesh that she would stroke with gentle hands, as though to soothe the restless child.

They seemed to be waiting, Helena thought. Waiting for something, but what? Waiting for the rebels to reorganize? Waiting for the whites to find and defeat them finally? Helena began to wonder if she should leave them and try to find Mester Bødker again. Lodama had said she could go. She had freed her that day they fled the women's camp.

Asari worked on his carving, aloof. Lodama moved to a place deep within herself and brooded on her unborn child. Only Lille was as she had always been—wide-eyed with wonder at the clanking progress of a hermit crab, chuckling with delight at the shining pattern of a spider's web splashed with sudden sunlight, or cuddling contented in Helena's arms in the evening, her thumb in her mouth.

Perhaps I will take Lille with me and go tomorrow to find Mester Bødker, Helena thought rebelliously. But she did not go; and one by one, the days passed.

When they had been camping near the pools six days, the message drums spoke. Asari raised his head to listen, his hand poised in midstroke as he sharpened his knife. Lodama, stirring the crayfish stew that cooked on the coal pot, tensed and turned to look at him. Helena saw the look that passed between them and put her hand over Lille's mouth to quiet her chatter. The drumbeats throbbed, and Helena thought Asari and Lodama had surely ceased to breathe, they were so still. The blood seemed to drain from their faces, even as she watched.

As the last beat died away, Asari put his hand over his eyes. The queen lifted her face to the sky and wailed a single, throbbing, high-pitched cry.

"What is it?" Helena said. "What say the drums?"

Asari lowered his hand to reveal his stricken face. He swallowed once or twice and moved his mouth as though to speak, but Helena heard no sound. When finally he began to talk, his voice was solemn and halting.

"The noble Kanta has . . . returned to the land of his ancestors . . . by his own hand. Ten of his people . . . among them the woman Bomboe . . . have . . . chosen to go with him."

"The home of his . . . Africa, you mean? They have gone to Africa? But how?"

Helena felt bewildered. Africa was across the sea. The rebels had no ships.

Lodama said, "They go as the little boy did go, but *they* chose their time."

Helena was growing impatient. "Speak plainly," she said. "Do you mean they are dead?"

Lodama bowed her head.

"They killed themselves," Asari said. "They chose to die . . . to end their lives free."

Lille seemed to understand the gravity of the moment. She laid her head in Helena's lap and sucked her thumb. Lodama swayed silently over the glowing coal pot.

"Oh," Helena said.

Helena thought about it. There was, it was evident, an alternative she had not imagined. It was not, after all, simply a matter of the rebels winning to make a new kingdom on St. Jan, or losing to be enslaved and tortured and killed. There was this third thing that could happen: the rebels could end their own lives as Kanta and his people had already done. Asari said, "chose." They "chose to die." Helena looked at the idea this way and that. It did not seem much of a choice to her.

"It's a stupid choice," she said suddenly as they sat that evening around the coal pot, eating their meal of crayfish stew.

Asari looked up.

"Dead isn't free," Helena said. "Kanta made a stupid choice." She clasped her hands around her legs and rested her chin on her knees. Her lower lip jutted angrily. "Stupid!" she said.

"Speak not of what you do not understand," Asari said quietly, and turned his head away.

Lodama did not answer at all. She gazed into the coal pot at the glowing chunks of charcoal and rested one hand lightly on her rounded belly.

Helena's heart began to beat rapidly. She jumped to her feet and kicked at the dirt floor in her anger.

"It's stupid!" she cried, and stumbled from the hut to pace the clearing in the drizzling dark.

And then, again, six days passed without event. They saw no one. They heard nothing. They slept and ate sparingly of Asari's dwindling supplies and tried to keep dry. Asari carved his curious symbols on the rocks, and Lodama grew even more silent, and Lille played with her pretty stones and shells or tried to catch the insects skipping on the pools. Helena's anger dissolved into unease. She woke often in the night to the thudding of her own heart and a kind of senseless panic, but she could not remember her dreams. Why don't I go, she thought. Why don't I leave them and go find my own people? But day after day, she stayed.

On the sixth morning, when she awoke, Asari was gone.

"Where did he go?" she asked Queen Lodama.

"To the king," Lodama said.

"But why?"

The queen did not answer.

"Soon, I make a birthing place," she said. "Today you shall help me gather palm branches."

"Is your baby coming?" Helena asked, suddenly excited. She remembered the night her brother Thomas was born. "But you shall need a woman to help you. I do not know about these things."

Lodama smiled, the first smile Helena could remember in a long while.

"An Adampe queen not need help to birth her child," she said. "It help gathering palm branches I need."

"But, is it coming? Is it coming *now*?" Helena asked.

"Not now, but soon." Lodama heaved herself to her feet. "Master Asari leave us his knife. Now, you shall fetch it, and we go."

They did not have to go far from the hut to find what was needed. Helena helped the queen bend down the fan-shaped fronds of the small silver palm trees so Lodama could cut them. She helped carry the awkward bundle of leaves to the hut.

Back at camp, Lodama took the largest, least ragged piece of linen to the pool and washed it. Helena was amazed at the queen's energy. She moved almost gracefully, and she laughed, actually laughed, at Lille's antics with a yellow butterfly. Something inside Helena eased. She found herself laughing too, a lightness in her chest. Even the weather sparkled, the sun shining in the afternoon with a brightness that steamed the rocks dry and warm. Together, Helena and Lodama spread the freshly washed cloth to dry and ate and stretched themselves to nap upon the warm rocks.

. . .

Helena woke to the touch of Lodama's hand on her face. " 'Lena," Lodama was saying softly. " 'Lena, wake you up."

Helena blinked sleepily in the golden light of the late afternoon and raised herself on one elbow.

"You shall come," Lodama said.

Helena saw that Lodama had the clean, dry cloth folded in her hand. She moved swiftly away, down the path toward the hut.

Helena scrambled after her. "What happens?" she said, catching up to the queen at the clearing's edge.

"I go now," Lodomo said.

"Now? So soon? Asari has not returned."

Lodama's eyes crinkled in a smile. "I not need Master Asari," she said.

"But . . ."

"I go. Now. Hear me well."

There was something in the queen's voice that stilled Helena's objections—a certainty, a command that Helena could not contradict. She listened.

"I gone all the night. Maybe . . . longer. You shall take care of Lille and wait for Master Asari."

"And you," Helena said. "When will you return?"

Lodama put her hand against Helena's cheek and looked into her eyes. "You a good girl, child. You a good servant . . . more than a servant to me. You a good little mother to children who got no mother. In time to come, you a good woman—a brave-hearted woman with hands strong for doing what must be done."

Helena felt the panic of her nightmares rising inside her. Lodama's words had a finality that frightened her. "You *will* return?" Helena cried.

Lodama was gathering the bundle of palm fronds. She slung them on her back and looked at Helena for one long moment more. "Do not forget this time, child," she said. "Do not forget Lodama, the queen."

She lifted her head proudly and turned and walked away into the brush.

"Queen Lodama. Queen Lodama!" Helena cried. "Queen Lodama, let me come with you."

The queen did not turn, or even pause.

Helena ran a few steps, holding out her hands. Then something in the set of Lodama's shoulders above the swaying bundle of palm fronds drew Helena to a halt. Her arms dropped to her sides helplessly. She watched the queen disappear into the tangled green of the forest.

"Do not leave me," Helena said, but her voice was a whisper. "Queen Lodama, do not leave me alone again . . ."

26

Darkness

Night fell, sudden and smothering. It did not rain, but lightning arced among the clouds, illuminating the forest clearing with blue-white flares. Helena brought the coal pot to the doorway of the hut and kept watch beside its glowing coals. Lille whimpered whenever the thunder crashed.

Helena was not sleepy. She watched the lightning and soothed Lille when it thundered. She listened, straining her ears to every sound. Every rustling in the brush brought her alert for footsteps. Every night bird's cry sounded to her like a scream of pain.

Helena felt utterly alone. She thought of Lodama, who was also alone in the forest.

The night baby Thomas was born, old Frue Hendrichsen and Neltje van Stell and young Madame Castan had all been in attendance on Helena's mother.

The midwife slave, van Bewerhoudt's Gretje, had been sent by her mistress, and all the Sødtmann slaves were put to work heating great quantities of water in the cookhouse, or running to and fro to fetch what the ladies wanted.

The house had been lit as though for a ball, candles blazing in every chandelier and candlestick, cresset lamps flaring on the gallery. Helena remembered how Papa Sødtmann had sat on the gallery, complaining of the heat and the length of time it was taking and the loss of his good night's sleep, while her mother's screams shrilled again and again from the bedchamber window.

Helena listened and did not hear screaming this night. Either Queen Lodama had made her birthing place very far from the pools, or she did not scream. She has no help at all, Helena thought. She clasped her hands around her shoulders and shivered, though the night was stiflingly hot.

Why had Asari gone to King Bolombo? He will return, Lodama had said. But, why, why did he go? Helena forced her thoughts away from what felt like danger. He will return, she told herself. He *will* return, and so will the queen. Mama did not return, said a small, frightened voice in her mind. Asari and Lodama *will* come back, Helena told herself. They will, they will come back!

Lille had gone to sleep. Helena pulled the pallet near the doorway and put Lille on it. Helena sat on the edge of the pallet, leaning her head against

the doorway, and rested her hand on the sleeping
child. The tiny, warm motion of Lille's breathing
comforted her. When Lille stirred, Helena stroked
her gently.

The lightning moved away across the sky. The
periods of darkness stretched longer and longer between the flashes, and the thunder rumbled ever more
faintly. Helena was glad it was not raining.

She tried to make plans.

If the soldiers find us, I will tell them we have
been hiding here all the while, Helena thought. I
will tell them Asari and Lodama had no part in the
rebellion. . . .

Helena remembered Mester Bødker had seen
Asari in the rebel camp.

I will say they helped me, Helena thought. Indeed, they did. I will say they saved my life. It is the
truth. I will plead for their lives. Perhaps Mama could
be persuaded to buy Queen Lodama and her baby and
Lille and . . . We could all live together at Coral
Bay . . .

Helena tried to imagine things back the way they
had been. She tried to picture Asari dressed in his
green livery coat, his eyes lowered humbly as he
waited for orders. She tried to picture Queen Lodama
—they called her Judicia when she was a slave, Helena
remembered. She tried to picture a docile Judicia
going about household tasks. Her imagination failed.

What will happen? Helena thought. What will
happen when the soldiers find us?

Helena dozed. She knew she had slept because, when she opened her eyes, the moon was up. She crawled out the doorway and tilted her head back to watch it sail across the sky—sometimes misted with wisps of flying cloud, sometimes clear and luminous against the star-sparkled blackness, sometimes ducking out of sight behind thick thunderheads. Finally she lay back upon the ground, the better to see it. She slept again.

It felt like a dream—opening her eyes to Asari's dark face, lit by the flambée-stok he held.

"You are back," she said. "Good. You are back."

Asari wedged his torch between two rocks and sat down beside her. He moved stiffly, like an old man, and his face looked drawn and ill in the flickering light.

Helena sat up. She glanced through the doorway of the hut. The torchlight fell on the small lump on the pallet that was Lille, sleeping. "The queen bears her child, Asari," Helena told him. "She went away this afternoon. She would not let me go with her. She said to wait."

Asari nodded tiredly.

"What will hapen to us, Asari?" Helena said. "What shall we do?"

"We shall wait," Asari said, and closed his eyes.

The next time Helena woke, she was on the pallet in the hut, Lille curled warmly against her. Doves complained in the gray morning mist. Helena could hear Asari moving about outside. It was a comfortable sound, and Helena closed her eyes, not ready yet to arise.

The day limped by.

Asari left for a time in the early morning, but returned soon with a pouch of hermit crabs, which he put to boil over the coal pot. When they were cooked and cooled, he pulled them from their borrowed shells. They smelled delicious, and he let Helena and Lille eat a few shreds of the meat as he cracked the claws, but most of the meat he saved and mixed with the last of the moldy millet to make a thick soup. "For the queen," he said. He spent the rest of the day at the pools, carving the rock, despite the steady drizzle.

Lille was fretful because she could not play outside the hut without getting wet. Helena tried to tell her stories, but her heart was not in fantastic accounts of an imagined future, and she could not remember Lodama's Anansesem tales.

At dusk, Lodama appeared on the edge of the clearing. Helena realized she was there when she heard a faint, mewing cry. She looked out the doorway of the hut and saw the queen steadying herself against a tree trunk with one hand. The queen's belly was flaccid above her loincloth, which was bound tightly about her hips. A tiny bundle was slung at her breast in the cloth Helena had helped her wash the day before.

"Lodama," Helena cried, flooded with relief and joy. "Lodama, you have had your baby. Let me see!"

Her impulse was to throw her arms around the queen in a hug, but the impulse was checked by the way Lodama swayed on her feet. She was tired, and she probably hurt, Helena thought, looking into her drawn face. Helena put her arm gently around the queen's waist and pulled the queen's arm across her shoulder.

"Come," Helena said. "Come to shelter. Come."

She staggered beneath the weight of the queen as she led her to the hut.

Asari was there by the time they reached the doorway, come running from the pools at Helena's cry. He helped the queen to a pallet and began to rub her dry as he had the first day in this camp.

"You did speak with the king?" Lodama asked weakly.

Asari nodded. He untied the sling from around Lodama's neck and handed the mewing bundle to Helena.

"And?" the queen said.

"Ya," he said. "On the morrow, it shall be done."

"I may join him?"

"You . . . and I . . . and many of his people."

"Good." Queen Lodama sighed. She brushed her hand across her eyes. "Good," she said.

Helena cradled the bundle on her arm, startled by its lightness and the tiny movements it made. She scooted to the coal pot and took the steaming vessel of soup from it so the glow of the coals lit the hut. Then sitting back on her heels, she laid the bundle on her knees and drew the cloth away.

The baby's head was small and round, covered with a soft fleece of curly black. Its eyes were closed, lashes feathering black on chocolate cheeks. Its nose was a soft, round button, its lips pink and delicately pursed. Two tiny, fragile hands waved on wrinkled wrists like sea anemones.

"Oh," Helena breathed. "Oh, my!"

Lille was enchanted by the baby. She could not be enticed away from it. She put out a tentative hand again and again to touch its soft cheek and squealed and retreated a short way, laughing, overcome by her own temerity.

"Lille Barn," she said, pointing to the baby. "Little baby." She pointed to herself. "Stor," she said. "Stor Lille. Big Lille." She drew herself up, then collapsed, giggling, into Helena's arms.

"Stor Lille indeed!" said Helena, hugging her. "What a silly girl! No, you are still my lille Lille, my little Lille, no matter how tiny the baby is."

They laughed together. Lodama's smile warmed her face. Asari crinkled the corners of his eyes. Even the baby made happy, cooing sounds.

By the time they had eaten the soup, night had fallen. It was a heavy darkness, thick with rain that pattered against the roof of the hut. But inside the hut, the coal pot glowed, and the food was hot and good. Lille and Helena were hungry, but Asari made sure there was plenty for the queen. When she protested she could eat no more, he said, "You shall need strength for the journey."

Helena busied herself with wiping Lille's chin. She did not want to hear.

Lille climbed into the circle of Lodama's free arm, when the queen put the baby to her breast. Lille snuggled against Lodama's side and closed her eyes.

Helena watched, fascinated, as the baby learned to suckle. At first it did not seem to have the knack, but patiently, Lodama guided the little mouth to the firm, brown nipple until it took hold.

The warmth of the hut made Helena's head heavy, but she did not want to sleep. She looked at Lodama's tranquil face, at Asari's, touched by gentle weariness. All the people I love are here, right now, she thought, and felt a little guilty at the thought. But Mama and Thomas and Bedstefader were so far away. She could scarcely remember them. She blinked her eyes wide, trying to hold onto the warmth and the safeness. Her eyes would not stay open. Struggling still, she felt them close.

"I rest a time," she heard Lodama say, and her head against Asari's arm, Helena felt him nod.

"They will wait for us," Asari said.

There was something Helena wanted to ask him, something important, but she could not remember what.

"I ready soon," Lodama said, and Helena fell asleep.

27

Daylight

She could hear them moving about, talking softly, as she came to consciousness. Her old, familiar, nightmare panic gripped her. Paralyzed, she could not move her hand or even open her eyes. Her heart was thundering so she could not make out their words. But she knew.

They were going. They were going without her!

She felt Asari's hand, shaking her gently. "Missy Helena," Asari said. "Awaken, Missy."

With an effort, she opened her eyes, and what she saw in his face made her close them again quickly. "Nej," she said.

"Awaken, Missy." His voice was soft, but it commanded her.

"Nej," she said, and forced her eyes open and struggled to sit up. "Nej."

"You must hear me, Missy," Asari said.

"I don't want to," said Helena.

"You must."

She stared at her hands, helpless in her lap.

"We go now, Missy."

"I know," she said, and her voice was angry.

"When daylight comes, go back to your people," Asari said.

Helena's head flew up. Her eyes were wide. "You do not take Lille with you," she cried.

Asari hesitated.

"Nej," said Lodama's quiet voice. "We not take Lille, child."

Helena's eyes swung to the queen's face.

The queen leaned forward and placed her bundled baby in Helena's arms. All Helena could see in her eyes was sad determination.

"Before time," the queen said, "I think I take him with me. But I find . . . I cannot. I think he have no good kind of life in this land . . . but I give him that life, and I must let him keep it . . . if he able."

Tears started in Helena's eyes, and she fought them back, angrily. "If he can live, why can't you?" she demanded.

"Missy . . ." said Asari, and his voice had a warning sound. "We do what we must do. It is not yours to question."

"You are giving up," Helena said. "You said you fought for freedom . . ."

"Dying a kind of freedom," Lodama said. "We weary."

"You are giving up. The rebellion is a failure,

and so you are giving up. They will say you were cowards. All this will have been for nothing!"

Helena lowered her head to shield herself from their eyes. She felt a touch and pulled away, trying to close her ears to Asari's voice.

"Fighting for freedom is not wasted," he was saying, "no matter how it ends. For half a year here on St. Jan, black people were free, and that is *not* nothing. It is night now, and we cannot see through the darkness, but daylight will come. We know it. The sun will climb in the sky, however slowly. And *that*, Missy, is something! I do believe the time will come when the land is bright!"

Helena felt him turn abruptly and knew he had stooped through the doorway and left the hut. There was a coldness beside her where he had been.

Lodama's hand was on her shoulder, insistent. In Helena's arms, the baby moved, his tiny legs kicking against his bindings with feeble thrusts.

"He the son of a queen and of a king," Lodama said. "He born free. Remember this and tell him."

There was a lump in Helena's throat that cut off her breath and voice. She raised her head, fighting to speak, but Lodama's hand was gone from her shoulder.

"Oh, Queen Lodama," she moaned.

But Lodama was not there to hear.

Helena was alone in the hut, alone with the sleeping little girl and the newborn child.

Gray ash smothered the heat of the coals. Helena's hand moved to pick up a green stick to stir them with, even before her thoughts began to move again. She was cold, she realized; the skin of her arms and legs were rough with gooseflesh. She looked to make certain Lille was warmly covered: The baby was a snug bundle in Helena's lap. Helena bent over him, warming herself for a moment against the heat of his tiny body. Then she laid him beside Lille on the pallet and added a few lumps of charcoal to the pot.

She wiped her hands on her shirt and hunched over the pot, staring into it as though to will the new charcoal to catch fire from the old, red-glowing coals.

Now, at last, I can go home, Helena thought, treading warily past a deep knowing place at her center. Perhaps Mama will still be glad to see me. When daylight comes, I will . . . What? What will I do now? Something inside of her was crying. Helena hugged herself hard to stop the trembling. I will go down to the shore where my people can find me, Helena told herself firmly. They will take me to Mama and home.

Lille stirred in her sleep, flinging one arm out of her linen covering. Helena reached to tuck her in, and her hand stopped in midair, wavering above the sleeping child.

Her careful thoughts plummeted to the deep knowing at her center. Home will not be the same, the knowing said. *I* am not the same, she thought.

Her hand moved again, and she watched it, surprised to see how steadily it pulled the linen cloth over Lille's shoulder, how it moved to brush Lille's hair in a gentle caress and came to rest, sure and quiet, on the tiny mound of the baby's bottom. It was such a thin, brown hand, Helena thought. She gazed at the calloused palm, the scarred back, the ragged nails.

She remembered how her hands used to look, turning the pages of her book or wielding her embroidery needle.

I never would have dreamed, Helena thought, those soft white hands could sweep or hoe or mend a hut's thatched roof. I never would have dreamed they could gather food or soothe a sleeping child. And now, Helena realized, she could not imagine her hands idle in her lap against a silken petticoat or fluttering a folded Chinese fan.

Helena lifted her hand from the baby and held it before her. She remembered Lodama's prophecy, "In time to come, you a brave-hearted woman with hands strong for doing what must be done." Helena turned her hand slowly in the red glow of the coals. It *was* a strong hand, she saw.

The baby whimpered, turning his head from side to side searchingly, and his mouth made soft, sucking sounds.

Helena bent over the children again. Gently, she touched the baby's satiny cheek with one finger. The free-born son of a queen and a king, she thought. Impatiently, she brushed away the useless tears that blurred her eyes. She did not know how she could see that he grew up knowing it, but—I will try, she thought. If I cannot find a place for myself—for them

—somewhere in the world, I will have to try to make one.

Helena took a deep breath and peered past the rosy glow of the coals to the doorway of the hut. Outside, slowly—so slowly Helena was not absolutely sure it had begun—the first faint flush of light grew in the sky.

Afterword

One hundred fifteen years after the St. Jan Rebellion, there was another organized and relatively successful slave revolt in the Virgin Islands. As a direct result of the demands of *those* rebellious slaves, the Danish Governor General Peter von Scholten freed all the slaves of St. Jan, St. Thomas and St. Croix in a proclamation read from the walls of Fort Frederik on July 3, 1848.